REMINISCENTS

A BLUE QUILL CHAPTER ANTHOLOGY

VIRGINIA BABCOCK   R. E. BEEBE   MEGAN CONDIE

J. ALAN GIFT   LEA GRAND   KAM HADLEY   LEO KEITH

K. HERRING   TERRA LUFT   INNA V. LYON

WM DAVID MALLERY   SEPTEMBER ROBERTS

VALARIE SCHENK   CALLIE STOKER   CRYSTAL L. VAIL

Blue Quill Chapter

ReminiScents

Copyright 2022 by Blue Quill Chapter

bluequillutah@gmail.com

Cover art copyright 2022 Dracon Studios

ISBN:9798371773197

"Dubois Ranch" 2022 September Roberts

"The Lingering Waft of Shadows (Of the Ghosts of Christmas)" 2022 Wm David Mallery

"Eucalyptus" 2022 Kam Hadley

"The Homestead" 2022 Crystal L. Vail

"That New Car Smell" 2022 Leo Keith

"I Changed Me" 2022 Virginia Babcock

"Moving Blues" 2022 Lea Grand

"Trace Amounts" 2022 Terra Luft

"I Remember" 2022 R. E. Beebe

"The Resistance, A Love Story" 2022 J. Alan Gift

"Autonomy High" 2022 Callie Stoker

"Mermaid's Justice" 2022 Inna V. Lyon

"Plums and Cherries" 2022 K. Herring

"The Humble Earthworm" 2022 Valarie Schenk

"The Smell of Books" 2022 Megan Condie

LEAGUE OF UTAH WRITERS

BLUE QUILL CHAPTER

The Blue Quill Club was founded on June 3rd, 1928. In 1937, when the League of Utah Writers was formed, the Blue Quill Club became the Blue Quill chapter, the League's oldest chapter. While many years have gone by and some things have changed, the core values of our writing group have remained the same. We, like other chapters of the League of Utah Writers, offer friendship, education, and encouragement to the writers and poets of Utah. While most of our members live in and around Ogden, we have members who travel for miles to join us. Everyone is welcome to attend our meetings. Whether you're interested in hearing from our guest speakers or participating in our critique groups, there's something for everyone in the Blue Quill chapter.

A Blue Quill Chapter Anthology

Book Four of Six

ReminiScents

Edited by Thoth Editing

CONTENTS

DUBOIS RANCH

SEPTEMBER ROBERTS

Paranormal Romance

*O*f all the ridiculous things Anthony had endured for his job, a team-building retreat might be the worst yet. He had deadlines and clients waiting, which left virtually no time for this nonsense. He also didn't like the idea of being away from the city, where he knew how to keep his urges under control. Despite his attempts to talk his way out of it, Mrs. Brown insisted.

And that was the end of it. No one questioned the Chief Financial Officer.

But that didn't mean he would be happy about it ... or participate. All he had to do was show up, greet everyone, then disappear to his room where he could work in peace and quiet.

The other accountants and certified public accountants who worked for their small firm had left in a rental van late that afternoon. Anthony had missed it by six hours, which is why he was stuck driving the nearly two-hour trek from Spokane, Washington, to middle-of-nowhere northern Idaho by himself. Not that he wanted company. Between the anxiety over work and his general grumpiness, no one would want to be around him anyway.

As the sounds and smells of the city slipped away, giving rise to the sharp bite of wilderness, the tension in Anthony's shoulders grew. All he could think about was the brochure Mrs. Brown handed him. In a cliché western font, Dubois Ranch boasted about horseback riding, building projects, sleigh rides, obstacle courses, and more! It was the exclamation mark that got him. He had strong feelings about people who used exclamation marks.

In the darkness of night, he listened to his GPS for directions and watched for anything that might dart out onto the road. He chewed a piece of peppered beef jerky, the spice helping to mask the wild smells surrounding him. The muscles in his back eased slightly, so he ate another. An entire package of jerky later, he faced a deeply grooved dirt road cut between thick trees. With a deep sigh, he left the last remnants of civilization.

Within a few minutes, a rock gouged the undercarriage of his car. Then a second and third. The fourth was accompanied by a string of foul language. By the time the lights of a distant house came into view, Anthony's anger had reached its peak. He finally pulled next to the van, got out, and dropped to his hands and knees. The gravel dug into his palms, making him itch to go for a run. He craned his neck to look under his car.

"Everything okay?" A man's voice interrupted Anthony's rumblings about awful roads, the cost of alignment, and the likelihood of leaking fluids.

Anthony got to his feet, his frown deepening. "No. Your road sucks."

The man narrowed his eyes. "That it does. That's why I stick to horses. You must be Mr. Orson. We expected you hours ago." He pushed his hand out, and Anthony shook it reluctantly. "My name's Jesse. Everyone else is tucked away for the night, but I can show you to your room. Follow me."

Anthony grabbed his things and directed one last scowl toward the road before following Jesse into the house.

A few feet down the hall, Jesse stopped and gestured toward an open door. "Here you go."

Peering into the room, Anthony scoffed. "Is everything cowboy-themed here?" Horseshoes and rope hung from the walls, and tiny horses galloped across the big rustic bed. Even the rug depicted a scene of cowboys swinging lassos overhead. Absolutely everything screamed yeehaw. Probably with an exclamation mark.

"You got a problem with cowboys?" Jesse asked, straightening to his full height, drawing attention to his ornate boots, worn jeans, and shiny belt buckle.

In a fight, Jesse would be a formidable opponent. But he was no match for Anthony, especially not in his true form. He wished this guy would just leave already.

"No."

Jesse nodded once. "Well, goodnight, then. Breakfast is at the big house at seven sharp. Don't be late."

With that, he left.

In a matter of minutes, Anthony had complained about the road, made fun of the accommodations, and insulted Jesse while sizing him up for a fight.

Perfect.

The agitation he worked so hard to control all the time spilled out of him. He walked outside, and the gentle sounds of night called to him, begging him to give in. "Screw it."

He undressed in the shadows of a big tree and shifted. Power coursed through him as his muscles thickened and his broad back sprouted black fur.

Victoria

"HEY, Frankie, can you come grab one of these?" Victoria struggled to balance three heaping platters and get through the door to the dining area unscathed. Hearing Frankie humming in the other room sent relief flooding through her. She always said yes to too much, and today was no exception. One mention of their cook's headache this morning, and she had added 'make a huge breakfast for guests' to her already full to-do list. But being busy beat the alternative. Frankie popped her head into the kitchen, her fine braids sliding across her face. She tied them in a knot at the base of her neck and smiled. "You bet. How much food did you make?" She took the platter of eggs.

"A lot? I don't know how much these people will eat. Louisa said to make the works, so I made the works. She knows best."

They went into the dining room, where they placed the plates of food onto warming trays next to the others. Victoria fussed over the food while Frankie finished setting the table.

"Morning, Vic. Morning, Frankie," Jesse called as he joined them.

Frankie tackled him with a hug that made Jesse's smile widen. Victoria already had a special place in her heart for Jesse, and when his niece joined them last summer, her heart grew a little bit more.

"Look at this. I'm as tall as Victoria."

Jesse tilted his head. "Vic isn't exactly—"

Victoria lifted her eyebrows, unable to keep the amusement out of her voice when she said, "Not exactly what, Jesse?"

"Towering."

"Are you trying to tell me I'm short?" She failed to smother a smile.

Frankie giggled. "I think he's calling both of us short."

"Rude. And to think I made a plate for you," Victoria teased. "With extra bacon and fresh honey on the biscuits."

4

Jesse took his Stetson off his head and held it over his heart. "When are you going to marry me, Vic?"

"That's the bacon talking. You don't want a bitter *short* lady like me." Not that Jesse meant it. They were friends and always would be. He'd seen her at her worst, when Victoria was still putting herself back together after Sal's death. She'd been grieving for years and kept waiting for the magical day when it would finally be behind her. One of these days. She was of two minds about the idea of being with someone again. It made part of her anxious. The other part, the lonely one, wanted to feel that connection again more than anything else, but not with Jesse.

"I never called you short." Jesse nodded thoughtfully. "Maybe a little height challenged."

"You better grab it before I change my mind and eat it myself." She checked her watch. "Guests should be here any minute."

"Mr. Orson finally showed up late last night. He's a piece of work."

More often than not, the city folks who came to Dubois Ranch were pleasant enough. But occasionally, a grade A jerk would show up demanding this or that. Like the whole world revolves around them. Who knows? Maybe it did back home, but not on the ranch. Victoria had lots of practice biting her tongue around people like Mr. Orson. "Thanks for the heads up. I'll be sure to give him the special treatment."

Frankie gave her a knowing look before disappearing into the kitchen.

Jesse nodded and grabbed his plate. "I'll be in the yard getting ready if you need me."

A few minutes later, the same group she'd met yesterday started trickling in. Victoria directed them toward the table overflowing with food. "There's plenty to go around, so eat up. You're going to need it." She counted the people in the room, reviewing their names in her head. Malosi with his warm smile, Ari with their flash of purple hair, Tanya with her dark round eyes, Sveta with cheekbones for days, and Rod in a different Hawaiian shirt but the same relaxed posture. No Mr. Orson. "As we discussed yesterday, today will involve—" Her sentence stuttered to a stop as a brooding, muscular man pushed his way inside the dining room.

"Morning, Anthony," Malosi said between bites. "Nice of you to join us."

Anthony grunted and slid into a chair. "I overslept."

"And you clearly woke up on the wrong side of the bed." Malosi smiled.

But his warmth didn't do anything to change the energy in the room, so Victoria spoke up. "Please help yourself."

Anthony scowled at her and didn't move.

"Unless you need to be served?" She lifted one eyebrow in challenge. The faint sound of Frankie's giggle came through the closed door to the kitchen.

"I can serve myself," Anthony grumbled.

"Be my guest." She held out a plate and waited for him to take it. For a big man, he moved gracefully. Almost fluid. It seemed at odds with the stiff, formal clothes he wore. Buttoned-up long-sleeve shirt, tie, slacks, and shiny black shoes. The rest of the team wore clothing suited for what would turn into a warm, sunny day. But not Mr. Orson.

He struggled to tug the plate out of her hands. Admittedly, she had been holding it a little tighter than necessary. Oops.

"There are still plenty of eggs and bacon, plus biscuits with honey from our hives last fall." She uncovered the jar of honey and smiled. Last year had been a good harvest. Beekeeping was a passion that not only fed everyone but also made her feel connected to the land in a way nothing else did.

With his lips pressed together, Anthony took a deep breath, probably in exasperation. Suddenly, everything about him changed. Just before he closed his eyes, they glinted a deep amber. The hard planes of his face softened as a deep rumbling sound came from his chest, something like a purr.

Anthony

WHAT IN THE world was going on with him? After keeping everything together for so long, control seemed to be something he didn't have in this place. He hoped his run last night would soothe the animal inside him so his rational mind could take over again. Nope. Something unsettled him here. The sweetness of honey lingered in the air, reminding him of a time when he'd been wild and free. The hot, tight feeling of the shift bloomed across his back. It took everything in him to stop it.

Shaking the memory out of his head, he squeezed his eyes shut, willing them back to normal. When it was safe, he looked directly into the woman's eyes. "I can take it from here." His voice came out low and rough as he grabbed a bottle of hot sauce.

"Suit yourself." The corners of her mouth lifted in a barely restrained grin as she covered the jar of honey. This woman, whoever she was, didn't seem to be intimidated by him one bit. "As I was saying," she said with a pointed look at Anthony, "today's activities will focus on teamwork on the obstacle course."

The image on the front of the brochure popped into Anthony's mind. People laughing and running, laughing while riding horses, laughing over meals. It made him suspicious of whether those people had been drugged. Anthony took his heaped plate and sat in his chair, his back to the woman. Something about her made his skin hum. That couldn't be good.

"Six is a great number for teams. Malosi and Sveta, you're the captains. Pick your teams."

Malosi grinned. Of all his coworkers, this man was the closest to a friend. Nothing ever dampened his good mood, and Anthony liked being around him, even if he kept that fact to himself. Malosi pointed across the table. "Ari and Rod, you're with me."

"Be prepared to lose," Sveta said with a smile as she turned toward Tanya and Anthony. "We can take them."

Anthony shook his head and doused his eggs in Cholula, trying to numb his sense of smell. "I have work to do."

"Mrs. Brown gave clear instructions. Everyone has to participate," the woman said. "Enjoy your breakfast. If you have any questions, I'll be in the kitchen."

Anthony turned and glared at the door she'd just walked through. "Who does she think she is? I never agreed to this."

"That's Victoria, and your work will have to wait," Sveta said. "Now, we focus on winning."

It DIDN'T MATTER how hard they tried; Sveta's team lost nearly every part of the obstacle course. Everyone welcomed the break for lunch.

Anthony grabbed a sandwich and stalked toward a patch of grass in the shade. Over the last few hours, his clothes had gotten rumpled, his shoes scuffed, and his mood was worse than ever. He scowled as he loosened his tie, dug a piece of jerky out of his pocket, and popped it in his mouth.

"We're not scheduled to start again for another twenty minutes or so if you want to change into something more comfortable."

Anthony glowered at the woman from earlier. Victoria. He hadn't packed comfortable clothes; he'd packed work clothes. "No, thank you."

"Suit yourself." At that, she burst into laughter. "Dang, that's funny. Get it? You're wearing a suit. Maybe that's why I keep saying it." Her shoulders shook with laughter and the strands of hair around her face glowed like honey in the sun. Soft lines deepened around her eyes, making her more beautiful than ever.

Her ridiculous jokes and beautiful hair were enough to push him over the edge, shifting his bad mood into anger. "Don't you need to be in a kitchen somewhere?" Once those words came out of his mouth, he realized how awful they sounded.

Her laughter died with one final snort. "You know, I always expect city folk to be more evolved than us country bumpkins, and time and again, people like you prove me wrong."

"I didn't mean it like that," he mumbled, having the sense to be ashamed.

"I don't suppose it matters how you meant it. I can take a hint." She nodded at him and walked toward the big house.

Victoria

AS EVERYONE FINISHED EATING DINNER, Victoria stood near the head of the table behind Anthony. After their brief interaction, she didn't want to look at him again, so this was perfect. Why did he have to be so rude? And why did it bother her so much? "I'm sure you're all exhausted after today's activities, but just in case, I'd like to warn you about the bears."

Anthony stilled and said in a slow, calm voice. "Was there a sighting?"

"No, but black bears are common in these parts, especially around food or garbage cans." As she spoke, she kept an eye on Anthony, who seemed to relax with each word. "If you plan on going out at night, be sure to go out in a group, and don't stray too far. We'll get a chance to explore some of the acreage over the next few days together."

While she cleaned up the kitchen, she couldn't shake how strange and calm Anthony's voice had been when she'd mentioned the bears. Or the way he'd looked at her that morning, like he'd been waiting for her to cower in his presence. Not likely. With her mind wandering, she pushed out the back door and smacked right into him, causing her to drop the bundle she'd been holding.

"Oh, sorry. I didn't mean to make you drop your ..." he trailed off, tilting his head to examine the contents. "Plastic bag full of raw meat?"

She snatched it out of his hands, her fingertips brushing his warm skin, sending a zing of electricity through her. She hadn't felt anything like that since Sal, who had been kind and loved her. This guy was a jerk, and she hated jerks. Flustered, she shook her head and grabbed the shotgun out of her office. "I need to go feed the animals before it gets dark."

He frowned, and his shoulders tensed. "Horses don't eat meat. Who are you feeding?"

"It's interesting you used the word *who* and not *what*. Most people don't think of animals as individuals." She narrowed her eyes and pushed past him, hoping to shake him off. The last thing she needed was another confrontation with this man, or worse, another one of those ridiculous thoughts about his hands.

"Wait up." He fell into step beside her. "I want to apologize."

"For asking inane questions?"

That stopped him momentarily, but he continued behind her as she marched through the meadow. "No, for what I said earlier about you being in a kitchen. That was rude, and I'm sorry."

Her heart raced. "Apology accepted. Now, please leave me

alone." With a quick glance over her shoulder, she could tell he had no intention of doing that.

He brushed her arm lightly and softened his voice, "I know you have a shotgun, but you just said it's not safe to go out alone. There are bears out here. So, where are *we* going?"

She let out a long sigh and refused to be touched by the concern in his voice. "Just to be clear, I don't have a problem with the bears. They usually mind their business. I actually think they're kind of cute. Most times, a warning shot in the air is enough to scare them away if they get too close to the house."

"Cute?" He snorted.

"Yeah, have you ever seen a bear? They're adorable. I kind of want to hug one, but then I'd probably end up dead, so that's not a good idea."

A bark of a laugh caught her by surprise. What was so funny? Fine, hugging wildlife did sound a little ridiculous.

"Ignore me. I don't have a filter around you. To answer your question, I'm going to feed the foxes."

"Foxes?"

"Yes, about this high." She gestured to her knees. "Red. Fluffy tail. Sharp, pointy teeth."

"You raise foxes?"

With another sigh, she turned around and started walking again. "No. I don't raise foxes. I do happen to live on a big patch of wilderness, though, and I know there's a den full of kits not too far from here. They were getting into the hen house before I started feeding them. Now, they don't. These are scraps anyway." She held up the bag. "No harm. No fowl." Unable to help it, she started laughing quietly.

It took a few seconds for recognition to light up Anthony's dark eyes before he rolled them. "Are all your jokes that bad?" The scowl nearly disappeared from his face.

"I thought it was good. What can I say? You bring out the funny in me." It had been years since anyone had put her at ease

11

enough to joke. Not since Sal. For the second time that night, she had to brush aside thoughts of Anthony like that.

As they approached the den, Victoria slowed and checked the direction of the breeze, adjusting their approach. "Stay here downwind. The mama tolerates me, but I don't want to spook her."

Anthony

ANTHONY DID as he was told and hunkered down. Victoria's soft voice carried on the breeze over the meadow along with the sweetness that lingered on her skin. A few minutes later, the smell of raw meat mingled in and became too much. His vision sharpened, and he knew the shift had started without his permission yet again. Breakfast had been a close call. Everything about this place tempted him.

"It's okay, you know me. I'm not going to hurt you," she soothed to the foxes, slowly crouching near the base of a tree. "How are you? I hope your babies are healthy. You are hungry, aren't you?"

The sweet sound of her words calmed him enough to ease the tension in his back and legs. Anthony sighed, and a contented rumble escaped his throat. The fox froze and made eye contact with him, growling before darting inside her den.

Victoria left the rest of the meat outside the den and continued to speak in that sweet, baby-soft voice. By the time she reached him, Anthony's eyes had returned to their human form.

"I don't know what got into her. I've never seen her so skittish." She frowned and glanced back at the den.

"How long have you been feeding her?" That seemed like a safer conversation than one about why a fox would growl at Anthony.

"Since February when she and her mate settled here." A soft smile tugged at her lips.

"Most ranchers probably aren't too kind to predators." He knew all too well the fear people had around anything they considered dangerous, whether they were or not.

"They belong here just as much as I do. Besides, I'm not like most ranchers."

He believed it. He'd never met another person like her.

DETERMINED NOT to be late to breakfast, Anthony arrived ten minutes early. The expectation of seeing Victoria again made his steps a little lighter. Instead of finding her, he met a woman in her sixties pushing through the door separating the kitchen and dining room.

"Where's Victoria?" He tried to look through the swinging door.

"Somewhere doing something. Bless her for stepping in yesterday. She's busy enough without having to do my job too."

Breakfast went smoothly, but he felt Victoria's absence.

She finally appeared when everyone had nearly finished eating. A red sting marred her perfect golden neck, and a frown creased her forehead. "You're going horseback riding today. Fill up your water bottles, grab a snack, and meet Jesse in the barn in fifteen minutes."

She left without making a bad joke or even smiling. By the time he got outside, she had daubed mud against her neck.

"Are you okay?" He motioned to her neck. What was it about this woman that made him care so much? Maybe he just wanted to hear the soft voice she'd used last night.

Instead of answering with sweetness, her voice was curt. "I got stung by a bee. Jesse is waiting." She motioned for him to join the others in the barn, but she hung back, clearly avoiding the place.

The aroma of fresh hay and warm animal filled his nose as he approached. Everyone except Jesse had already mounted their horses.

"Let's get you settled on Peaches." Jesse tugged on the reins of a light brown horse, but she whinnied nervously.

"Horses don't like me."

Jesse frowned. "Peaches is usually calm. I don't know what's gotten into her." He reached into a bag on his saddle and gave Anthony a carrot, directing him to hold it out to her in his open palm. Instead of taking it, Peaches took a few steps back.

Embarrassment heated his cheeks. He should've expected it, but the fear in the horse's eyes made him acutely aware of exactly what he was. Could the others see it, too?

"What's the holdup?" Malosi asked from the back of his horse. "You're not trying to get out of our daily team-building activities again, are you?"

Anthony rubbed the back of his neck and looked away. The last thing he wanted to do was make Peaches uncomfortable. Well, more uncomfortable. And now everyone was looking at him, and he had to fight hard not to run away.

"We'll take the shortcut," Victoria said from far outside the open barn door, without stepping inside.

"Vic, are you sure?" Something passed between them, and Anthony couldn't make sense of it.

"I'm sure. We'll see you there for lunch, okay?"

Jesse mounted smoothly and nodded, then he clicked his tongue and led the rest of the guests out of the barn, the teenager with the braids trailing behind on a smaller horse with Peaches in tow.

Anthony closed the barn door and fought the urge to run. He quickly joined Victoria.

"Let me change my shoes. I'll be back in two shakes of a

14

lamb's tail. Meet me at the big house?" Victoria gave him a reassuring smile and jogged away. A few minutes later, she returned wearing hiking shoes and holding a pair out to him. "These should fit you."

"I don't know what's going on." The urge to run still controlled him.

"These activities are required. Your boss was very clear. The fact that the slowest, oldest horse in our barn didn't want anything to do with you isn't your fault, so instead, we're going to hike to meet them, and you can't hike in those." She tapped her foot against his dress shoes.

The more she spoke, the calmer he became. "And you just happened to have an extra pair of hiking shoes my size hanging around?"

She nodded but didn't elaborate. "We better head out."

For the first time this weekend, he wanted to thank his boss for making activities mandatory. He couldn't think of a better way to spend the day. After quickly packing a bag of supplies, she started up a hill behind the barn.

"Why did Jesse sound so worried about you taking me?" he said when he caught up.

"I'm not great around the horses, so I was going to leave today's activities to him. Besides, I need to catch up on last month's receipts and expenses for the ranch. It's my least favorite part." She took a deep breath and blew the air out of her cheeks.

Anthony nodded. "You cook and do the books?" He couldn't help being impressed. He'd never met someone as capable, kind, and, he begrudgingly admitted, funny.

"I'm a Jack of all trades, what can I say?"

"I'm an accountant. Let me help you." Before Victoria could protest, Anthony went on. "I insist. I'm interrupting your day, so let me repay you. Tonight, after dinner." Any excuse to spend more time with her was just fine by him.

Victoria pressed her lips together and nodded. "That would be nice. Thank you."

The gentleness of her voice soothed him, and he wanted to hear more of it. "How did you get stung?"

"I was doing an inspection in a couple of the hives this morning." She pointed south, where a meadow sprawled near the garden. A dozen square structures dotted the soft grass inside a tall fence. "The ladies were grumpier than normal, and one decided I was a threat. It always makes me so sad when one dies because of me. They make me so happy most of the time." She touched the side of her neck gingerly. "It hurts like the dickens, but the rewards are so sweet. Literally." She opened the bag slung over her shoulder and pulled out a jar containing a piece of honeycomb. "See?" With a swift movement, she popped the lid, and the fragrance of honey surrounded them.

Just like that, he was a cub, sitting on the front steps of the cabin with his dad, licking honey off his paws.

Victoria

"ARE YOU OKAY?" Victoria stared up at him, catching a glint in his eyes. She'd noticed it the first time she met him. A flash of color. But just like the first time, it disappeared as quickly as it had appeared.

"Yeah. Good. I'm good." Anthony cleared his throat and took a step away from her. He pulled a pouch of jerky out of his pocket and stuffed some into his mouth. "You're not allergic? To the bees, I mean?"

"Heavens no. I would be a sad beekeeper if I were."

"It would be unfortunate."

"Indeed, it would." She smiled at him, hiding behind the rim of her hat as she admired the way the sun made his black hair shine and softened the grayish tinge of his taupe brown skin. "I should've checked on them a little earlier. They're too active once the sun is up. Plus, they're still on edge from the skunk who got inside the fence. Tomorrow is supposed to be warmer, so I'll go earlier. I had to be sure they were okay. Everything looks good, though, so I got stung for nothing. Well, not *nothing*." She tilted the jar toward him. "They made comb where they shouldn't have, which is why I broke it off. Silly girls. They made this piece with nectar collected from the lavender growing on the edge of the garden. It's delicious." She narrowed her eyes at him. Every time she nattered about bees or foxes or the ranch, he seemed to relax, but then he had moments where he seemed coiled tight, like a spring. Like he couldn't stand to be around her. "Do you like honey?"

Anthony swallowed hard and nodded but didn't look at her. "Very much."

Despite his words, he made no attempt to take the jar she offered him, so she put it back in her bag and started walking again.

The trail the horses took looped the long way around the property. Their path would lead them directly to the picnic grove.

When they stopped to drink, he said, "These shoes are comfortable."

The fact that another man wore Sal's shoes should've bothered her, but it didn't. She couldn't think about that for too long. "Good. You can keep them."

"They must belong to someone. Won't they want them back?"

Victoria shook her head. "They were my husband's. He died seven years ago, so I'm pretty sure he won't want them back."

Anthony stilled and turned to look at her, his eyes filled with remorse. It was at that moment she realized why she went out of her way to spend time with him. The softness buried inside this hulking man made her melt.

17

"I'm so sorry," he whispered. He reached out toward her but seemed to change his mind and let his hand fall by his side.

"Me too." The truth kept coming out of her mouth. "He used to wrangle the horses. Sal was careless. Thought he was invincible. Got himself killed." She didn't like to think of that day, even now.

"Is that why you avoided the barn?"

She nodded slowly. He'd noticed? "Not that I blame the horse. I was so mad at Sal for leaving me." Tears pricked the corners of her eyes. "I don't know what's gotten into me. I think my filter is broken."

"You have a filter?" The slight teasing tone in his voice put her at ease.

In all the years of counseling, she'd never been able to admit how angry she was at Sal. And here she was, spilling her guts to a stranger. But Anthony didn't feel like a stranger, not really. She hadn't opened up to anyone like this in years. "My therapist said I should face my fears. I haven't been in the barn since the accident. I haven't been able to. It's called exposure therapy, and it sounds awful."

"Maybe it wouldn't be so bad if you didn't have to do it alone."

She could swear her heart stopped beating. "What are you saying?"

"I'll go with you." He shrugged like he was offering to carry her bag. No big deal. Except it was.

"You would do that for me?"

Another shrug. "Of course."

"You're kind and a good listener."

"Listening is easier than talking. Especially with you," he added quietly.

They got to the picnic grove nearly an hour before the rest of the group, giving Victoria time to sweep off the tables and benches with a bunch of dried grass stalks held tightly like a broom. Anthony followed suit with his ever-present scowl etched deeply between his eyes.

The horseback party arrived, and the afternoon unfolded, filled with structured activities led by Jesse. Although she watched with the pretense of getting to see Jesse in action, which she didn't have the opportunity to do often, she spent most of the time watching Anthony. She'd never seen someone enjoy beef jerky so much. Like each bite had purpose. More than once, their eyes met, like he couldn't help but watch her too. He was like a knot she'd spent all day trying to unravel. A man of few words and even fewer facial expressions, she couldn't stop thinking about how safe she felt around him. Not to mention the other feelings. The ones that stirred a longing so deep she didn't recognize them at first.

But they were there. The desire to touch him burned deep inside her, which is exactly where it would stay.

During their return walk, Victoria's stomach twisted in knots. Maybe Anthony wouldn't remember his promise to visit the barn with her. Maybe she could just walk back to the big house and spend the rest of the afternoon doing something else. Anything else. A root canal would be preferable.

The barn came into view, and her breath caught.

"Are you okay?" Anthony stopped walking.

Finally, she looked up at him. His usual scowl had been replaced by a gentle, concerned look. It soothed something inside her. She nodded. "I'm okay."

"We don't have to do this. We can just sit here and wait for everyone else to come back."

She didn't want to do it, and he was giving her an out. Exposure therapy seemed like a terrible idea. Who needs closure? Not her. No, sir. She could go on living her life avoiding the barn and all the horrible memories held inside.

Or, with Anthony's help, she could take a deep breath and face her sorrows. Her therapist wouldn't lead her astray, would she? Would going back in there really help her heart heal? There was only one way to find out.

Anthony broke through the silent battle in her mind. "If you're not ready—"

"I'm ready." She nodded and walked with deliberate steps toward the barn. Anthony kept up with her, and her shoulder pressed against him, grounding her and helping her put one foot in front of the other.

With Anthony by her side, Victoria pushed the barn door open. The late afternoon sun poured inside, and a mélange of horses, hay, aseptic medicine, and the ever-present aroma of manure wrapped around her, squeezing her chest. It had smelled just like this seven years ago. The day she didn't want to remember. She had gone to the house for just a few minutes. Just long enough for Sal to get hurt.

Tears slid down her cheeks. She stepped inside on shaking legs. Anthony wrapped one warm hand around her elbow and squeezed gently. She gave him a watery smile.

His touch never wavered. It gave her strength when she thought she would fall apart. They walked the length of the aisle toward the last stall. The mesh door, like all the rest, was open, inviting her inside. She knew the rubber mat and bedding had been replaced, but that didn't stop her eyes from searching for the pool of blood.

"We'd just gotten a new Quarter Horse," she whispered. "He was a nervous little guy. Especially at feeding time." With trembling fingers, she reached toward the edge of the feeding trough. The edge of the metal seemed smooth enough, but it had been sharp enough to cut through skin and bone. "Sal insisted on calming him down. He knew it wasn't a good idea, but he went inside anyway."

Anthony stepped closer, giving her a place to lean. It felt right to have him there. He didn't say a word, leaving plenty of space for her to continue talking.

Her knuckles turned white as she gripped the unforgiving metal. "The horse spooked and tried to get out. Sal hit his head." The words barely came out of her tight throat. She slid to the floor as a sob wracked her body. Anthony went down with her, his warm, protective body pressed against her back, supporting her while her grief tore her apart.

They sat like that for a while, the sound of her sobs filling the quiet space. She wiped her face and took a deep breath. "Sal was trying to help."

"He sounds like a good man," Anthony whispered, his breath warm against her neck.

"He was. I miss him." She took a deep, shuddering breath. "He didn't mean to leave me."

"I'm sure he didn't."

She breathed deeply, letting go of the pain inside her and replacing it with the knowledge Sal would never have left her intentionally. That he loved her and was trying to do a good thing. A good thing that went horribly wrong.

After another few minutes of breathing, she finally cleared her throat. Her therapist had been right. She hadn't felt this peaceful since before the accident.

"Thank you for being here with me."

In response, he squeezed her arms.

"I'm a mess," she said with a weak laugh, looking down at her dirty hands. The same hands she'd used to wipe her tears away. "Come on, let's get out of here." She held her hands out to Anthony. They walked outside and headed to the spring that fed the pond a hundred yards away. Victoria dipped her fingers into the cool water of the stream and rubbed vigorously. She splashed her cheeks and dried her face on the sleeve of her shirt.

"Do you feel better?" He glanced toward the barn.

"Yeah." She meant it. "Thank you for helping me."

He gave her a soft smile, and it made her heart beat sideways.

She leaned over where the spring came out of the ground and filled her bottle then did the same for Anthony.

"This spring is the reason my great, great, great, great grand-père settled this land."

Anthony's eyes widened. "This is *your* land?"

Victoria laughed. "I didn't take Sal's last name when we married; it made more sense to keep the Dubois name. We were one of the first French-Canadian families who settled the Idaho Territory. Whose did you think it was?"

"Jesse's?" he said with a shrug, then his face stilled. "That's why you're doing the books, taking care of the bees, cooking, and everything else. You must have so much on your plate. I don't think I can fully express how grateful I am for you spending today with me. Thank you."

Breathing became very difficult. The sincerity in his voice did funny things to her stomach. The day had been a mixture of awful and wonderful. It had been awful to relive those horrible memories, but wonderful to be with Anthony. She stood and held out his water bottle, looking up into his eyes. "Thank *you* for spending the day with *me*. It means more to me than you know. I don't take as much time off as I should. What's the point of living in all this beauty if I don't stop to appreciate it every once in a while?"

"What time should I stop by?" He didn't move to take his bottle. He didn't do anything but stand there, breathing hard and looking at her mouth.

Stop by? For what? All she could think about was how wonderful it had been to have this man all to herself. Especially when he looked at her like that. And he wanted to stop by to see her again.

Oh. Her hopes squished like a piece of honeycomb. He was stopping by to help with paperwork. "Eight? I'll be in my office just outside the kitchen." When she placed the water bottle into his hand, her fingers grazed his heated skin, stoking a flame inside her. "I'm looking forward to it. Thank you for offering." Before she could do anything preposterous like kiss him, she walked toward the big house to help Louisa with dinner.

Anthony

ANTHONY WATCHED Victoria as the early evening shadows of the house engulfed her. Energy hummed through him, fed by a day spent with that delicious, vulnerable, kind, and trusting woman. He had to hold it together. Just a little longer.

Everyone sat around the large dining table that night, eating, laughing, and talking about their day out. Victoria ate quietly, keeping her eyes downcast for most of the meal. She had been through so much that day, and she'd let him be a part of it. He'd watched her fall apart and put herself back together. Had she noticed the way he had been looking at her all day? Could she see the yearning in his eyes? Did she know how powerful her touch was? Simultaneously calming him and driving him wild.

He watched the clock and counted down the minutes until he could be alone with her again. Everyone cleared out after dinner and went their own way while he took a deep breath, stuffed the last of his jerky into his mouth, and calmed himself before knocking on the door outside the kitchen.

"It's open," Victoria said. She sat at a desk, her head bent over an open ledger and a stack of papers.

Anthony walked in and tried to ignore the sweet smell he associated with her, concentrated in this small, cozy room. "Put me to work."

She stood and motioned for him to take her chair, which still held the heat of her body. "I've been going over these figures for the last half hour without much progress." She rubbed her face and stretched her neck, letting out a long sigh.

All he had to do was focus on the numbers. Not her. Not the

way her skin glowed in the soft light or the way her golden hair framed her face. Just numbers. Numbers were safe.

"I got stuck here," she said as she reached across him to point at a receipt.

He gripped the edge of the desk, his skin hot and tight. "Could you ..." What? Stop smelling so good? Stop talking and kiss him? "Get me a glass of water?"

"Oh, sure." Victoria frowned but left the room.

Anthony let out a sigh of relief and focused on the work in front of him. He bit into a peppercorn that had gotten lodged in his teeth, relishing in the sharp, earthy taste. Over the next hour, he tried to stay on task and mostly succeeded. He had to send her on several more errands, asking for things he had no need for. Something, *anything* to put space between them. He clearly hadn't thought this through.

"That would've taken me days." Victoria leaned over the desk, looking over the page he'd been working on. She grinned at him, a dimple showing in her left cheek. "You're amazing. You know, there are a lot of folks in town who would happily hire you to do that. I'm one of them."

Anthony held her eyes and tried not to look at her mouth. Or the soft hollow at the base of her throat. "I just," he started and shook his head. "You're welcome." He cleared his throat. "Good night." He couldn't get out of her office fast enough.

In his room, he paced from side to side. The last hour had been sweet torture, and there was only one thing he could do to get her out of his mind.

Anthony slipped outside and started shifting before he could get his pants off. The seams of his shirt ripped, and buttons popped off as his chest and arms expanded, leaving a trail of torn fabric toward the pond. The ground still held the heat of the day, but when his paws touched the water, it quenched the fire inside him. He took a deep breath and ducked under the surface, coming up a few seconds later to float on his back, his paws spread wide.

A chorus of crickets sang around him as the moon appeared overhead, blazing a lazy path in the inky sky. The stillness was interrupted by an explosion that jerked Anthony back to his human form. There, standing on the edge of the pond, a shotgun pointed at the sky in one hand and a pile of clothing in the other, was Victoria.

Her mouth hung open. Her eyes wide. The gun fell to the ground just as everyone from the house spilled outside.

Anthony scrambled to his feet, digging his toes into the soft mud at the bottom of the pond. The night air on his shoulders and chest reminded him why he couldn't leave the safety of the water. He held his hands up in surrender. Oh, no. No. This wasn't happening. This couldn't happen. His life was over. His job, his security, everything he'd so carefully built. Done. All because he couldn't control himself for two days.

Jesse arrived first, breathless and frantic. "Vic, what's wrong? What happened?"

Victoria turned to him slowly and seemed to take in the scene from Jesse's eyes. She smiled and touched his arm. Even in the darkness with his human eyes, Anthony could see the smile was forced. "I thought I saw a bear. My mind is playing tricks on me. Can you take the guests back inside and send Frankie out with a towel?"

"You got it." He nodded and narrowed his eyes at Anthony. "You sure you're okay?"

"I'm sure. Thanks for checking on me. Will you take this in?" She bent to pick up the gun and handed it to Jesse.

Once they were alone, Victoria turned her attention to him. "You can put your hands down; I wouldn't have shot you. Or anything. Not even a bear." A frown creased her forehead.

He took a step closer, the cool night air stealing heat from his hips. Her eyes slid down to his exposed abdomen, and a blush colored her cheeks.

She looked into his eyes, and the frown deepened. "I can't understand what just happened. It isn't possible ..."

"Victoria, please." He begged for his safety, his future, his life.

"What's the ruckus all about?" the teenager with the braids asked as she jogged toward them with a towel.

The same tight smile stretched Victoria's face. "Nothing, just a guest going for a late-night swim. Thanks, Frankie."

"You're welcome. Do you need—"

"Thanks, Frankie," Victoria said pointedly. The kid got the hint and ran back to the house. In a harsh whisper, she went on, "I came to check on you. You left so abruptly, but you weren't in your room. I found these." She held up his tattered clothing. "Then I saw a bear, and I thought you were hurt. Then I saw ... you." She shook her head vigorously.

"Victoria, please," he begged again.

"I don't know what I saw or what to think, but I do know I need some time to process." She placed the towel on the ground and walked away.

Victoria

IT ALL MADE SENSE. No, it didn't. None of it made sense. Bears didn't turn into people. That didn't happen in the real world. But it had. Victoria had seen it herself. One second a massive black bear swam in her pond, the next, Anthony stood there in all his muscular, naked glory. His usual scowl replaced by a look of sheer terror.

He was afraid of *her*.

Even after the long day she'd had, sleep did not come that night. Well before the chickens announced the new day, Victoria dressed and started her chores. Her footsteps faltered as she approached the meadow with the beehives. Anthony sat with his back against the fence, eyes closed, face tilted toward the lightening sky.

He blinked and looked at her with the same fearful look in his eyes he'd had last night. "Can we talk? I couldn't sleep."

"Neither could I." Victoria lifted the lid on the closest hive. "I'm listening." With a tiny crowbar, she quickly separated the frames in the super, checking each one against the pale sky. Beautiful cells of capped honey nearly filled each one. A few bees landed on her, disturbed from their slumber. "Good morning, ladies. Don't mind me." She kept her voice soft and low.

Anthony came up beside her, his usually tidy shirt untucked and unbuttoned to his collarbone, dark hair peeking through the opening. "Aren't beekeepers supposed to wear a suit of some kind?"

She shook her head. "Only when I split a colony, and the girls are good and angry. Usually, they're calm like this." Satisfied with the state of the frames, she replaced the lid and turned to him.

"I can see why. It must be your voice. It's very soothing."

She tilted her head and noticed how relaxed he looked in that moment. "You wanted to talk about last night?"

He looked away and twisted his hands like a little kid who had gotten caught doing something they weren't supposed to. "I'm sorry."

"What happened? I still can't wrap my brain around it."

"What do you think you saw?" He looked at her for a split second, then away again.

"A bear. I saw a big ol' black bear in my pond. I thought it had killed you. But it *is* you, isn't it?" Her heart hammered in her chest. These were the impossible thoughts that had kept her awake all night. When he didn't respond, she went on with a laugh, "But that's ridiculous. People can't change into bears."

"Yes, we can," he said quietly.

His words stunned her into silence. Her mind spun. Anthony could turn into a bear. No way. How could she believe him? That wasn't possible, was it? She should've run screaming, but she didn't. All she could do was think about how exactly that would work. She had so many questions.

"Please, don't be mad," he whispered. "I'll leave now. But please, don't tell anyone."

She tilted her head up toward him and frowned. "Mad? You just told me you can turn into a bear, and you think I'm mad?" A smile split her face. "That's the most remarkable thing I've ever heard. Also, you're scheduled for a full day of activities, so you can't go yet." If she was honest, she didn't want him to go. Ever.

He opened his mouth, but nothing came out, so he closed it. He did that several times with the same result.

"I'm fascinated. Tell me about yourself. Do you have family?"

Anthony shook his head. "My mom left when I was a baby, and my dad died years ago. That's when I moved to Spokane. I couldn't stand to stay in our cabin in the woods without him. I don't date, I don't have friends, and my apartment sucks."

"Oh, you poor man. You're all alone in a city where you can't be yourself. No wonder you're so—"

"Uptight? Grumpy? Cantankerous?" He supplied these words with a straight face.

A laugh bubbled out of her and, to her surprise, he joined her. He smiled and laughed. A genuine sound of joy. "That sums it up nicely." She touched his arm gently. "Maybe you should try a change of pace. Dubois Ranch seems to suit you."

His face went still, and his throat worked. "It's more than the Ranch that suits me."

Heat burned her cheeks. Was he implying what she thought? "Thank you for trusting me with your secret."

"Thanks for not freaking out." His shoulders relaxed, and his smile softened.

"Believe me, I freaked out plenty last night. I thought for

sure I was losing my mind." Now she had questions. "How does it work? Can you do it now?"

A flush spread up his throat and across his dusky cheeks. "Not if I want to keep my clothes intact. My body gets a lot bigger. Some might say cute or adorable." He gave her a pointed look.

She laughed as she remembered what she'd said to him. About wanting to hug a cute, adorable bear. That was truer now than it had been then. "And furry, right?"

He nodded.

"Is it soft?" That probably sounded like she wanted to touch him to find out. She did, but he didn't need to know that. She couldn't help but glance at the chest hair she could see and wonder the same thing. Heaven help her. "Ignore me. My filter is broken."

"You don't have a filter, remember?" He laughed.

"Hey," she said, trying to look offended. "I'm sorry for prying. This is all very interesting."

"I don't mind. Truly. The only person I've ever talked to about it was my dad, and he was like me."

"Cantankerous?" She grinned.

He gave her a deadpan stare. "Funny. No, a bear. It's nice to talk to someone about it. Turns out, you're a good listener, too."

"It's easy listening to you." Victoria moved to the next hive and struggled to remove the lid. After a few seconds, it gave way with a sticky pop. "Girls, I've told you to stop building comb on top like this." She held the lid out to him like a plate where the oozing mass of broken cells spilled honey. "Anthony, you need to taste this."

He lifted the piece into his mouth and groaned.

When their eyes met, she saw the familiar flash of amber brighten his dark irises. "Your eyes. They did that thing again."

"The shift is hard for me to control sometimes. The honey doesn't help."

Realization dawned on her. "That's why you didn't want it yesterday when I offered. I thought maybe I'd said something wrong."

He shook his head. "You didn't do anything wrong. In fact, the only reason I'm holding it together at all right now is because you're talking to the bees in that soft voice. It's very soothing."

"It's funny. Sometimes you look at me like that, like you're about to fall asleep. Other times, you look at me like ..." she trailed off, unable to think of the right word. She chewed on the piece of comb left behind in the hive, licking the honey off her fingers. When she looked at him that time, his eyes were solid amber, and he remained perfectly still, watching her mouth with predatory attention. Before, she had interpreted this look as irritation, but now she saw it for what it was: Anthony about to lose control. Because of her.

Anthony

THIS WOMAN. Did she know what she was doing to him? "We should go in for breakfast."

"Anthony?" She took a step closer to him. "Are you okay?"

Definitely not. "Yep."

"I'm curious. What would happen if I kissed you right now?"

A soft growl escaped his throat, and when he spoke, his words came out raspy. "Aren't you afraid?" He could hurt her. Didn't she realize that?

"Of you?" She shook her head, took the lid out of his hands, replaced it, and stepped even closer to him. She laced her fingers through his. "I trust you."

His heart stuttered. The way she touched him, with such kindness, made him think maybe he could have a normal life. A life *with* someone. A life with her.

He leaned forward and pressed his lips to hers, and his brain went still. Nothing had ever been so sweet. When they pulled apart, she smiled up at him.

"You didn't change. I thought—"

A surprised laugh escaped his lips. "I didn't know what would happen either. I haven't tried that before. Also, this is not how I imagined this conversation would go."

She tilted her head. "Oh? What did you imagine?"

"Screaming? Running to get your shotgun? Neighbors with pitchforks?" That last one was a joke. Sort of.

"You're not a monster. You're a marvel." She stood on her toes and kissed him again. That time, he wrapped his arms around her waist and pulled her tight against his body. It felt right. It felt like home.

THE LINGERING WAFT OF SHADOWS (OF THE GHOSTS OF CHRISTMAS)

WM DAVID MALLERY

Personal Essay

"Melancholy is the happiness of being sad." — Victor Hugo

I grew up in Florida and have never known the smell
of chestnuts roasting on an open fire.
Christmas always smelled of salt and sand.
I finally discovered the crisp, clean scent of a White
*   Christmas at age 56.*
At that time, I had traveled to Utah from Mississippi,
where I led a state agency responsible for long-term
*   disaster recovery.*
I served in the position throughout the
Hurricane Katrina and Deepwater Horizons disasters.

I hope your holiday memories hold no haunting
from the smell of sour devastation after a hurricane,
or the permeating stench of a massive oil spill,
or the metastatic odor of cancer.
I struggle to forget them.

Nowadays, I gaze at winter's majesty
through our own window to Christmas on Mt. Ogden.
My personal notes from these separate occasions don't
    make a perfect story.
But life isn't perfect.

*M*y First White Christmas
          There is an inescapable melancholy that is
part of Christmas. It is a shadow of the ghosts of Christmases
Passed, writ large on our present. No matter how much we
enjoy the season, there are always songs and smells and tastes of
Christmases long ago that we attach to memories of yore. Great
memories. Mostly. Most of us were, at one time, children impatiently excited for gifts beneath a tree. As the years pass, our
lives evolve. The child in each of us lives on, but we are increas-
ingly burdened by worries and frets and the busyness of life.
Deep inside, we don't really age. We learn. Often the hard way.
We like to think that we become wiser, but perhaps we only fool
ourselves with veiled attempts to harden to the mold of
adulthood.

But this time of year! The Christmas songs and lights and
the smell of evergreen boughs—these things reach beyond the
hardness, jingling the bells of our memories!

And melancholy sneaks in. We can pretend it doesn't, but it
finds a way. Even Elvis had a Blue Christmas.

Along with each memory—however we may choose to
address it, embrace it, or hide from it—there comes a glow of
warmth in our heart-hearth. The memories become more
fleeting with the passage of time and years. I can attest to that!
But for their elusiveness, they become all the more precious to
us. And as ephemeral as the moment and memory may be—of
our own Childhood Christmas … or a lost parent or grand-
parent … or a memory of a child now grown and gone—each

has its shadowed ghost of sadness. And we realize that they are memories we cannot relive ... cannot recapture.

We (mostly) do not focus on the sadness in these reflections but rather on the heart-warmed goodness of the love and joy that the memories bring to us. But with each memory relived, beyond our periphery, the shadow of melancholy grows. The Ghosts of Christmases Passed whisper to us. Whether or not we want to hear them. These voices often echo from a cold, dark hearth when we are least expecting.

Or maybe it is just me.

I know irony. I believe that life has its yin and its yang. Hot defines cold. We learn to cherish love when we acknowledge things like hatred, fear, and selfishness in our world. Those memories, so beloved, bring the shadowed juxtaposition of those things that I have lost. My own childhood. My own children. My grandparents. My father. My brothers and sisters. Most recently, our family home in the country that defined "over the river and through the woods" in my mind and in my heart. (The old family place, built before the Civil War, was recently lost to fire.) Great memories, sure. But the images accentuate the absence ... Christmas Melancholy.

But I digress from the moment.

Shortly before we traveled to Utah for my first White Christmas, my phone rang. I saw the name on the display. It was someone I cared a lot about but who seldom calls me. A business acquaintance. But I am a fortunate person for whom "business" aligns with my life's passions. So, the term "business acquaintance" rarely works for me. She is family.

Her voice is immediately tired. As with all family members, we can sense when things are out of order. From that call, I learned that today her husband is having a lump removed from his neck. They already know it is cancer. They won't know until after Christmas how far the cancer may have spread throughout his body. Their family celebration has been juxtaposed by the dark shadow of Christmas Future. We will Pray for them. We will Hope. I sit here in my own irony at my wife's family home in Utah, watching the snow fall quietly in nature's solitude beyond a glass pane. No matter how hard my heart wishes, I cannot send to their hearts the bright tranquility that I see ... or replace their pain with my pane-view of flakes of peace ... in their white purity ... falling from the heavens.

Exactly one year prior to that call, I was preparing for a quiet Christmas when I received a different call. A late-night call from the Governor's personal cell phone was a rarity. Mother Nature had broken the peace ... had delivered to a community the devastation of the ghost of Christmas Present in a whirlwind that shattered Homes and Hopes and Dreams. Whatever else they may be, tornadoes are decidedly not Christmas gifts. In the darkness, I arrived in Columbia, Mississippi to see people's Christmas scattered across the dark, wet, devastated aftermath-landscape of the twister. That scene was most decidedly NOT Christmas. One by one, my calls were returned, and our loved ones were okay. But also, not okay. They responded, though, by becoming Santas for their whole community. Not just for the day, but for an entire season. Of recovery. One year later, I know they remember. And again, I wish that I could share with them the heart peace I now feel as I look up and again cherish the falling snow gathering on each branch. The boughs grow heavy and release their burdens in silence. Irony: The Ravages of Nature. The Peace she can bring.

Christmas Melancholy. Perhaps it is not something we should escape but rather part of the season we must embrace. There is joyous peace to be found in this world. But there is also cancer and loss and devastation—things that will find us.

Tears of love. Tears of joy. Tears of pain. Tears of loss. Tears of fear. These are not so different. Like hot and cold, they define one another. Without great love, the sadder things mean nothing. If I had not shed tears of love and joy for the time I had with my children, I would not recognize the taste of the salt in the tears of sadness now that they are gone.

For now, though, I cannot help but count the blessings that are my life: people and communities that I love enough to feel pain when they hurt. Christmas Melancholy is the ghost of a shadow. For the moment, I will conclude these thoughts and return my focus to the serene snowfall scene before me and the heart-warmth of my beautiful wife, patiently and lovingly sitting beside me as I write.

Right now.

This moment.

This is Christmas. The best of …

And I will wish for all:

Peace, Joy, Love, Healing, Recovery.

The memories of goodness when we taste the salt of sadness.

FIRST POSTSCRIPT: Reflecting on the Shadow of Christmas

Michelle's Mom lives on the evergreen steppes of the mountains in Ogden. Her living room has a big bay window. When we visit for Christmas, as we are now, her mom allows me to remove the curtains and sheers from the huge windows and turn the two chairs in the sitting area of the bay to face the wonderland outside. Here, Michelle and I sit with hot cocoa and freshly baked banana bread, and we prop our feet (in warm socks) on the windowsill. It is magical. Especially for a kid who grew up making sandmen instead of snowmen on December's balmy Gulf Coast. The songs of White Christmas and Winter Wonderland and Jingle Bells have attained new meaning.

Shortly after writing the previous essay, before dusk could settle fully on my peaceful wonderland vista, our Silent Night was shattered by another devastating December 23 tornado back in Mississippi.

How can that be? Before daylight the next morning (Christmas Eve), Michelle dropped me off at the Salt Lake airport, so I could return to Mississippi. It was to be our very first Christmas with our new granddaughter. Michelle did her very best to hide her tears as I walked away. She wiped her cheeks, thinking I wouldn't see. But her tears had already fallen on my heart.

SECOND POSTSCRIPT: Christmas as a Utahn

I cannot say that it was the never-ending challenges of facing communities again and again after disaster ... But ten years was enough. At least for me. More important is the fact that the people and places of Utah began to feel like a home that I missed when I was away.

We recently bought our "forever home" on Mt. Ogden and have settled in. Things aren't perfect just because we moved here. We've had a few earthquakes. During our first autumn, hurricane-force mountain winds brought our apples down for us. We are still working our way through a pandemic. Our views from Mt. Ogden of Ben Lomond peak and the Salt Lake Valley are often obscured by the smoke from myriad wildfires, bringing new smells and making new memories. Despite all of this, the old Christmas songs of yore hold new meanings for me.

Now, during the holiday season, the scent of snow and fire-wood and apple pie (our own apples!) help define my life in new ways. It is the smell of "I'll Be Home for Christmas." (And maybe someday we will roast chestnuts on the fire.)

EUCALYPTUS

KAM HADLEY

Contemporary Fiction

"Happy anniversary, Devon." My husband took my hands across the table, looking at me sweetly. The clatter and din of the restaurant receded as I gazed back at him.

"Happy anniversary, Ray." The lantern on the table flickered as I spoke. A shiver went down my back. Wasn't low lighting supposed to be romantic? Instead, it added to the eerie nature of this place.

As most of the city, Lamashtu catered to tourists seeking vampire lore. A repurposed Victorian mansion, it was all sharp angles and shadows. The waiter, dressed as a vampire, approached our table. Dipping his head to the side in a little bow, he said, "Good evening. My name is Isaac. May I get you started with something to drink? The Bloody Mary is to die for."

Ray squeezed my hand, spurting out a laugh. "Wow, you folks really go all out here with this vampire theme you've got going on."

Isaac smiled a small smile, his eyes flashing in the flickering light. He passed us each a menu. "I shall return," he said, then slipped silently away.

Opening the menu, I jiggled my shoulders in an effort to shake off the creepy feeling. This place was getting to me. Luckily, the food looked ordinary enough. Telling Ray my order, I excused myself to the restroom. I needed a moment to collect myself and, I admit, I hoped to avoid another encounter with Isaac so soon.

Using the restroom in public is a tricky thing for a nonbinary person. There is no right answer for which room to use. Good fortune was in my sights, though. This place had one large door, marked simply, "Toilets." Entering, I found it was actually a room with several small rooms inside it. Inside one of the smaller rooms was a toilet, a sink, and a small counter area. There was even a recliner. Odd. Everything was clean so, shrugging, I made my way to the toilet. I let the tension drain out of me as I went about my business.

Washing my hands, I noticed an extra soap dispenser near the sink. Something about it didn't look quite right, so I used the other one and left the room.

Exiting the toilet area, the dim lighting of the restaurant wrapped around me. Shivering, I turned to head back to my table when a little boy went running by. No one chased or followed after him, though he was much too young to be on his own. I paused, looking after him. Should I follow and make sure he's okay? What if he finds he's alone and gets scared? He might need help getting back to his parents.

Decision made, I followed the rambunctious, dark-haired toddler as he zipped down a hall. Turning the corner, the hallway darkened, but a light could be seen at the end, and that is where the boy went.

Rushing in after him, I came to a stop when I saw the boy holding on to the leg of a woman who looked just like him. She patted his head, placating him as she continued her conversation with a stunning man in a white lab coat. "Why can't you set up your own lab somewhere else?"

"That lab has an *apheresis*," the man hissed. Seeing me, they stopped speaking abruptly.

After a moment, the woman gathered her wits. "Hello. May I help you?"

"No, uh. Well, are you the boy's mother?" I motioned to the boy, toddling and playing nearby.

"Yes, of course. That is Benjamin. He's nearly three, and he knows this place as well as his own home. I'm Aria, the owner." The woman stepped forward, offering me her outstretched arm. As I shook her hand, her red fingernails poked into me just a little. It was nearly unnoticeable but was enough to be a warning to me.

Releasing her hand, I stepped back, nearly running into the man she'd been conversing with. As he stepped aside to miss me, a fresh smell swooshed around him. I wanted to breathe it in but was too unnerved by the restaurant owner. "I'll just head back to my table now." I motioned over my shoulder, then quickly turned and fled back down the dark hallway. I swear I felt them holding their breaths, watching me go.

Sliding into the booth, I struggled to calm my heart as Ray regarded me from across the table. Reaching over for my hand, he said, "Did everything come out okay?"

I tried laughing at the old joke, but it sounded strangled.

"What happened?" Ray asked.

I opened my mouth to respond when suddenly, Isaac was there. I jumped, but he set coasters and water glasses down as if it were nothing. Smooth as can be, he also placed a board with warm bread and soft butter. He looked at us and put the cutting knife on Ray's side. Perhaps he thought a jumpy person with a knife wasn't a good idea, but something about it rubbed me wrong.

Isaac slipped away, and I snatched the knife and started sawing at the bread.

"Devon, slow down. You're squishing it all up."

Shocked back to the moment, I looked at the mangled loaf. I dropped the knife and pushed the board across to Ray. My eyes shifted around restlessly as I slumped back into the seat of the booth. I didn't know if I could eat here, wound up as I was, but when my eyes caught sight of Ray watching me warily, I had to try. It was our anniversary, after all.

The meal came. It was tasty and normal.

Ray made casual small talk until I relaxed a bit. Just as we were finishing, Aria approached. "How was your meal?" she asked politely.

It was normal enough for a manager or restaurant owner to check in with customers, but the shrewd look in her eyes told me she didn't miss a thing. Her presence at our table seemed an ominous warning that she knew who I was and would not soon forget me.

Ray wrapped everything up and grabbed my hand. Stiffly, I followed him out, hoping never to return to that place again.

LEAVING my office at the university campus the next evening, where I taught and ran the lab, I made my way to the parking lot. It had been a long day. Sitting behind the wheel, I took a moment to stretch out the kinks in my neck.

Someone had been in the lab last night. Everything was neat and clean, but some of the beakers and burners were not where I had left them. Tonight, I took pictures of the lab when I locked up. Supposedly, I was the last one out and the first one in, so everything should be the same in the morning as it was the night before.

For a solid week, I took pictures every night, and nothing was amiss. Perhaps I was wrong. I snapped pictures one more time anyway, turned out the lights, and locked everything up.

Ray was sitting at the table, laptop open when I arrived home. "Devon, come look at this." Angling the laptop my way, Ray slid over so I could see what he'd been looking at. It was a news article.

Birth Blood Missing From Hospital, read the headline. The subtitle had me rolling my eyes. *Vampires in the city?* "What are you reading?"

"This is the *Gazette*."

"You've got to be kidding me. Maybe you clicked a link to a gossip magazine." Inspecting the browser, I discovered the article was indeed in the *Gazette*. "Huh. Missing blood?"

"Yeah, it's missing from the labor and delivery unit. According to the article, blood lost in birthing is disposed of, so this may have been going on for a long time without anyone catching on. Sometimes people bank their cord blood, but those also usually go to the incinerator. Everything is collected in special containers and transported to a disposal unit. At least, that is what is supposed to happen."

"It says here that the driver of the courier truck checked the order and discovered the pick up to be three containers short. *'It's not something we log or monitor closely,' the driver admitted.* I bet they'll be checking it more frequently now."

"Yeah, unfortunately, this feeds the vampire lore rooted here." Ray grimaced, taking his mug to the sink and rinsing it. "Are you hungry? I saved a plate of food for you in the microwave."

"Yes, please."

Shaking my head, hoping to clear out any distraction, I set to work grading papers and finalizing lesson plans for the next day. This city was full of vampire crazed tourists. Of course, the missing blood would be blamed on vampires. The hospital should be held accountable. "Back to work, Devon," I scolded myself.

The next morning, the lab had been disturbed again. Snapping pictures, I took note of specific items out of place: a beaker, a burner. The centrifuge seemed slightly off center, but the most noticeable thing was a missing vial rack. I hadn't thought to take enough pictures to inventory everything, but I knew a rack was missing. What was happening? Chewing my lip, I made my way to report this to the department head.

"Devon, welcome. Come in, you look troubled."

"Someone was in the lab last night." Thaddeus cocked his head, listening more intently, so I continued. "I locked up as usual last night, but this morning, things were out of place, and a vial rack is missing."

"The lab was ransacked?"

"No, it's all very neat and clean, but small things are not exactly where they were the night before. Here, I have pictures."

Accepting my cell phone, Thaddeus flipped through the photos while I pointed out the subtle differences in item placement. "Hmm. Yes, I see. What made you think to take these? You must have suspected."

"Yes, I noticed something off a week ago, so I started taking pictures each night when I lock up."

"Good thinking. It almost isn't noticeable. Only someone very familiar with the lab would have caught that. It's spotless, and everything is nearly where it was before."

"Yes, but what of the missing vial rack?"

"I shall check with security and see if we have camera footage of anyone coming or going. In the meantime, keep taking pictures." He passed the phone back to me. "Please email me the ones from last night and this morning."

"Okay, yes. I better get to class."

"Thank you, Devon."

A few days went by, and Thaddeus got back to me. Security

did not catch anyone on camera. Apparently, the system had momentarily "glitched." Coincidence? I didn't think so. Obviously, Thaddeus and Security couldn't keep my lab safe. That would be up to me.

"Artichokes, Mommy. Can we get some, please, please?" I smiled, hearing the little boy in the produce aisle begging his mom for artichokes. Kids who love vegetables are amazing. I put some broccoli in a bag and snuck a peek at the sweet child.

Sucking in a breath, I nearly choked on my own saliva. It was the same little boy, Benjamin, from the restaurant. The red claws gripping their shopping basket had me slipping away, hoping to remain unseen.

As I continued my shopping, I kept an eye out for the restaurant owner and her son. Mercifully, the boy's babbling chatter gave me enough knowledge of their whereabouts that I was able to keep my distance.

Grabbing the last of what I needed, I headed for the checkout. Of course, there was only one lane open. Taking my place at the back of the queue, I felt rather conspicuous. Darting my eyes about, I expected Aria and her son to come upon me at any moment. The line behind me grew as I neared the front. A second cashier came and opened the lane next to me just as I reached the front and unloaded my items.

"Artichokes! I want to put the artichokes on." I shivered, knowing who was behind me without even turning to look. My cashier scanned the items, but I was so tuned-in to the people at the next check stand that she had to ask me twice before I grabbed my wallet to pay.

Waiting for my receipt, I overheard a snippet of Aria speaking with her cashier. "My dear, when are you coming back to my place? Got to keep you looking young and ravishing now, don't we?"

Wait. People don't go to a restaurant to upgrade their appearance. Perhaps I misunderstood. I had only heard part of the conversation.

Tucking the receipt into my bag, I resisted the urge to sneak a peek at the cashier. I didn't want to take the chance of Aria recognizing me. The piercing gaze she'd given me at the restaurant still haunted me. Only when I pulled into my driveway at home did I breathe easy. Maybe I needed a vacation. Stress had to be getting to me. Surely, things weren't as odd as they seemed.

"Are you going to the party this weekend at Wyatt's? He's having a fire."

"No way. Not with all the vampires around here."

"You can't be serious."

"It's too dangerous to be out after dark. Haven't you seen the news?"

Students filtered out of the classroom, taking the conversation with them. I had half a mind to follow them, just to hear the rest.

Wiping down the counters and making sure everything was in its place, I snapped photos and locked the lab. I'd made it through another week and desperately needed the weekend break. Ray and I had plans to get away and attend a hot air balloon festival.

AFTER DRIVING FOR FIVE HOURS, the cliffs opened up, and we pulled into the rural destination town. We checked into our room and walked down to see the local tourist shops. The first shop was a jewelry store. A display front and center showcased necklaces made of garlic strands. Oookay. Never saw that one before. It had a hemp-like quality to it with the fibers pressed together. But the smell? Undeniably garlic. Why would someone wear that?

The next shop sold ornate and beautifully handcrafted rugs. Ray and I browsed the store, fingering them as we went along. The shop owner came to speak to us. "Hello, welcome. You are in town for the balloon festival?" We nodded, and he continued. "Ah, yes, and where are you from?"

"Wallachia."

The man gasped and grabbed my arm, tugging me toward some rugs across the room. "You need these. A dangerous place is where you live. These rugs are woven with garlic fibers right in them. The added protection they provide you will be invaluable. Let's see, you will need three? Or, how about four?"

Proceeding to pull rugs down for us, Ray and I watched the man in complete befuddlement. "Wait, wait," Ray spluttered at last. "What?"

The man looked over his shoulder at us, squinting. Turning, arms laden with rugs, he said, "We know all about the problems you have in Wallachia. Here, in Kent, we protect ourselves." He motioned with the rugs as if it were the most obvious thing in the world. Seeing the incredulous looks on our faces, the shop owner continued. "It works. We have no problems here with ...," he looked around furtively and whispered, "creatures of the night."

Ray scratched his head and looked at me. I widened my eyes and shrugged, gesturing toward the door. Ray turned back to the man. "Thank you for your kindness and concern. We will keep these things in mind."

"See that you do," the man shouted at our backs. "I will save these aside for you."

Leaving the shop without looking back, we hurried into the next place without checking to see what it was. Stopping short immediately, I grabbed Ray's hand. He paused and looked at me with shock mirroring my own.

Candles flickered in the dim interior. A large, glass display case sat in the front, but it was the mannequin off to the side that drew our attention. He was dressed stiffly, in a black suit with tails. There was a white dress shirt and, speared right where the heart of the person should be, was an ornate wooden stake.

Peering into the display case, we saw wooden stakes of all sizes in varying degrees of ornamentation. The shop worker was moving our way, but rather than get caught up with another kook, we fled the store.

"What kind of town is this?" Ray asked. Continuing down the block, we passed the next store without going in. The displays in the windows told us all we needed to know. Crosses in all sizes, from plain to bejeweled and fancy. Hurrying on, we made it back to our room at the inn.

Closing the door behind us, we sat facing one another on the bed. "Do you think it's worth it to stay?" I asked.

Ray massaged my knee. "Let's see the balloons in the morning. We both need a break. We can stay in our room tonight."

I agreed. We ordered pizza and watched TV. We gave each other back rubs and, in time, went to sleep.

The next morning, we were out on the field before sunrise. Several balloons were being laid out and prepped. One by one, they were filled and slowly raised off the ground. Vibrant colors and designs graced each one. There was Spiderman, a bumblebee, a ladybug, and a balloon with puffy fish poking out around the sides. They were so big! Teams of people were required for each balloon. As soon as one took to the sky, a truck left to follow and collect it wherever it ended up. What a way to travel. I decided then and there that I wanted to go in one someday.

On an adrenaline high and thinking perhaps we had misjudged this small town, we meandered back a different way to our inn. Turning up a new street, an odor assaulted our nostrils until Ray accelerated to get through it faster. Passing a processing plant, the source of the smell became obvious. Clusters of garlic hung, drying in large bunches. "This town! It ought to be renamed *Garlicville* or *Garlic Oasis*."

Ray agreed, chuckling as he stepped on the gas a little more. We checked out of the inn, foregoing the next two days we had planned to stay. If we were going to be inundated with vampire superstition, we might as well head home and rest in our own bed.

A NEW SEMESTER was set to begin. I had my haircut appointment today, and then I'd be ready. There hadn't been any more acts of vampirism in the news, nor had the lab been out of order in any way. Whatever had gone on months ago was clearly in the past. I hadn't even given it a thought until I was mid-cut.

A tinkling at the door signaled a customer entering the salon. The stylist paused snipping my hair to look over and welcome them in. I looked up, too, and caught my breath. Benjamin and Aria. That little boy! I dreaded the sight of him. His mother was never far away. Even the sound of his voice, chattering about getting his hair cut, grated on my nerves.

Another stylist came from the back room and seated Benjamin, putting a drape around his neck. Aria was distracted and didn't seem to notice me, for which I was grateful.

When my cut was finished, I followed my stylist to the desk to pay. I couldn't resist eavesdropping as I stood nearby.

"Aria, you are looking so good these days."

Aria ran a finger along her own jawline, gazing in the mirror. "It really does make a difference, doesn't it? I feel younger too."

With my transaction complete, I had no reason to linger. Not even curiosity could get me to approach and ask what they were talking about. Probably some new beauty product. Salons were all about those sorts of things.

Shrugging it off, I made my way home. The new semester would begin in the morning, and I wanted a good night's sleep to start it off right.

PEACEFULLY, in my dreams, I visited the lab. I had the place to myself, loving the quiet stillness. No distractions. I could take up as much space as I wanted. Safety goggles on, I moved about, immersed in my work. Rounding the counter for more supplies, a whoosh of fresh air came over me. Eucalyptus. That scent, like the swoosh of a white lab coat. The swoosh of a white lab coat!

Abruptly, the dream changed. I stood in the creepy vampire restaurant with Aria directly in front of me, along with the man in the white lab coat. That was where I'd smelled that scent before! He'd stepped aside to avoid a collision, and that lovely, fresh eucalyptus scent had swirled.

Gasping, I sat up in bed, images crashing through my mind. Misplaced items in the lab, blood missing from the hospital, the lab coat man conversing with Aria in the vampire restaurant. It was all connected. Flopping back onto my pillow, I stared at the ceiling.

How could I prove it? Should I pretend I know nothing? Getting involved would surely be dangerous. This was my lab, though. I had to assert responsibility. Gritting my teeth, I determined to go back where I'd vowed not to: Lamashtu.

LAMASHTU LOOMED BEFORE ME, gargoyles leering. Even though it was the middle of the day, darkness gathered here. I had come alone, but I'd left a message for Ray, who was working, so he'd know where I was. I told myself that by doing that, I was being brave and not stupid because at least someone knew where I was.

Throwing my shoulders back, I strove for an air of confidence. I didn't want my presence to be questioned. Walking in, head high, purpose in my steps, I made my way to the hallway I had followed Benjamin down before. The passage was dark, as previously, but this time, there was no light at the end. There was no one there at all.

I couldn't have come here for nothing. I was not giving up. Aria had to have an office around here. I just had to find it.

Taking an adjacent hallway, I slowed my steps, hearing voices ahead. A light shone out of an open doorway on the right. Creeping closer, words jumped out as voices escalated.

"I've almost perfected it. One more night in the lab might be all I need to collect enough hematopoietic cells. I am on the cusp of something that will change the world," a male voice declared.

"Yes, we will change the world, Troye, but it will be through my beauty transfusions." A female voice overrode the other.

Standing three feet down the hallway, I stopped in my tracks. This was the evidence I needed. Pulling out my phone, I thought to record the conversation. Before I could hit the button, though, Benjamin came out the doorway and saw me.

I held my finger to my lips, hoping he wouldn't give me

51

away. He went back into the room. I held my breath. Could I be so lucky? Still, I should probably not linger here.

Just as I thought it might be safe to move, Benjamin peeked around the corner at me. His smile grew when he saw me, and he quickly ducked back around. When he repeated the action, I realized he was playing peek-a-boo. This would give me away for sure. I had to get out of here.

"Aria, wait," the man, Troye, said.

I spun and retreated but was pinned against the wall quicker than I could get out of there. Aria twisted my left arm painfully behind my back while the man in the lab coat pushed against my back, smooshing my face into the wall.

"Benjamin," Aria hissed. "Open the bottom drawer in my desk and bring me the long white pokey things. Benjamin did as Aria asked, returning with zip ties.

I took a deep breath, intending to call for help, but Aria pressed her hand over my mouth. Her eyes bulged out in anger, red fingernails cutting into my arm and face where she held me. "Don't you dare make a sound," she threatened. She didn't give me a chance anyway, for as soon as the man had my hands tied behind my back, Aria took her scarf from her hair and stuffed it in my mouth.

The fabric quickly absorbed any moisture in my mouth, and I could barely breathe. As I forced air in and out of my nose, Aria and Troye each took hold of one of my arms and drug me up the hallway I had come down the first time. Upon reaching the restroom, Aria sent Benjamin in to see if anyone was inside.

"People gone-gone, Mama." Benjamin's sweet toddler voice caused my heart to plummet. I looked around frantically and tried kicking out to trip my assailants, but Troye picked me up and put me in the reclining chair inside the stall. Pulling a zip tie from his pocket, he zipped each of my legs independently to the metal of the extended footrest.

Thrusting my torso to and fro, I knocked Aria into the sink.

"Ooh, you're going to pay for that." Aria started messing with the thing on the wall that I had previously dismissed as an outdated soap dispenser. My eyes widened, and I nearly swallowed the scarf when she opened it and pulled out tubes and syringes.

"Which one are you going to use?" Troye asked.

"Does it matter?" Aria snapped.

Turning my head, I searched for Benjamin. He was gone. I tried calling out, but a muffled moan was all I could manage.

Troye pulled two vials from his pocket. Holding up the smaller one with clear fluid, he said, "Use this one first. Once they are sleeping, we can play." The sinister gleam in his eye, and the light glinting off the second vial of deep red liquid, caused me to panic further.

Aria took the vials, and Troye shoved me forward, folding the top half of my body over my legs that were extended and strapped to the footrest. My arms, zip tied behind me were now exposed. Aria snickered, snapping on rubber gloves and sanitizing my vein with an alcohol wipe. *Heaven forbid you be unsanitary now*, the voice in my head added sarcastically.

Aria tied a tourniquet around my arm. I tried to wiggle, but Troye held me firm, my face pressed against my knees. A sharp prick pierced my vein, and cold fluid was inserted. Aria fiddled around with the needle, leaving an IV port in place. Great. Now they could access my vein repeatedly.

My arms and shoulders felt heavy, and a dense fog pressed in my head. I blinked quickly, trying to hold off the effects of whatever they'd injected, but it was well and truly too late. I never should have come alone. Ray wouldn't get the message of my whereabouts until he got off work. By then, I would be long gone.

My eyelids closed against my will, and I sucked in a breath. A fresh eucalyptus smell filled my nostrils. That scent, once so clean and lovely was tainted, now sinister and dark.

THE HOMESTEAD

CRYSTAL L. VAIL

Adult Supernatural Fiction

*M*aggie tried not to feel the skeleton's toothy grin as she focused on the road ahead. She would not look at him today. She would not stare at his stark white bones. Maggie would drive her mail truck down the row of mailboxes and keep her eyes from drifting in his direction. If Maggie kept ignoring him, maybe he would go away.

Yeah, right. Maggie thought to herself.

She had worked the same mail route since she started thirty years ago, and every day he was there, leaning his boney elbow casually against a locked metal gate on the other side of the road. The gate was located halfway down a long weed-strewn driveway that ended at an empty lot surrounded by overgrown trees and shrubbery. Grass fields and distant farms were the only neighbors connected by a row of mailboxes on an old highway outside of town.

The lot hadn't always been empty. There used to be a two-story farmhouse with a large open attic and a balcony overlooking the front yard. It was built in the middle of the 1800s and had been home to multiple families throughout the decades.

Tragic accidents and strange deaths seemed to plague every family that lived in the home. The last owner walked out after his wife committed suicide. He left everything in the home. Rumors and legends grew over the years about what caused all the mayhem on the property. Teens pulled pranks around Halloween, and vandals cleared out the valuables before the city finally burned it down and removed all remnants fifteen years earlier. When Maggie dared to steal a look down the path, she could still see an outline of the home in the growth of the trees. It was actually a lovely home before it fell apart. She had secretly wanted to see the inside.

Maggie couldn't keep her gaze away and finally glanced at the skeleton for just a second. It was enough for him to notice. With his bleached fingertips, he tipped his black bowler hat toward her with a big grin of pearly whites. The years of standing against the fence had not inflicted any change or damage to his bones. His slight movements were smooth and deliberate.

On her first day of work, she noticed him and hid in the back of the mail truck for what seemed forever. Once her heart slowed down and her legs regained their strength, she peeked out the truck window and realized he had not moved. He was not coming toward her. He never moved. For thirty years, he had never moved from the gate.

That first day, she immediately went back to the post office and told her boss what she had seen. He stared at her and then laughed. He claimed it was just teens trying to scare passing drivers. He then became serious and reminded her she was on probation and that she better finish the route on time the next day. She finished the route and then returned the next day and the next. She was a single woman with no living family or support system to speak of and truly needed the job. The pay was good, and the benefits were needed. She knew she couldn't find a better job with her experience. It took a couple of months before she quit shaking and messing up the mail across from the homestead. She never told another soul. Nobody would ever believe her.

Seeing the skeleton was only part of the mystery. Every five to ten years, mail would be addressed to a Harold Krum at the same address. It was always a postcard with an early picture of the homestead on the front and just one line on the back, "Will you be attending? Yes or No." Every postcard had the yes circled with no return address. She would deliver the postcard, then check the mailbox the next day, and it would be empty. Someone always collected the mail. One time she saw a police car at the homestead, days after a postcard, but nothing was mentioned in the news.

The only solace Maggie held on to was that she was retiring at the end of the week. Her pension would be enough to take care of herself and two aging Siamese cats, Darcy and Sassy. Only one more week of not staring at the skeleton.

The next day, when she reached the homestead's rusted mailbox, her heart skipped a beat. The red flag was up, which had never happened before. She opened the box, and inside was a letter with no stamp and yellowed from age. She examined the envelope, and the return address listed the name Harold Krum. The mailing address was also just a name. A scream caught in her throat. Her own name was staring at her, in loopy black ink, Ms. Margaret Allred.

Maggie did not finish her route that day.

She arrived home hours before the end of her shift. Darcy and Sassy were sound asleep on the couch. They stretched and shared a drawn-out yawn. Maggie sat on the couch, and her furry babies wrapped themselves together by her side. She absently stroked their ears and stared at the envelope in her other hand. A battle arose within as to whether she should open it or burn it. She had read somewhere you shouldn't burn evil things.

It had to be from the skeleton? She thought to herself.

She tore a small part from the edge and then set it back down in her lap. If it was the same letter as the others, inside should be a postcard wanting to know if she would be attending. If she didn't open it, she would never know for sure. If she did open it, would she say yes? What happened to the others that responded? She never saw a report in the news, but she had heard rumors. Rumors of kids finding a body. Rumors of police not wanting to go out and check on the property.

Shadows developed from the sinking sun and filled the room. Only a small lamp provided light by the corner of the couch. Her kitties had finally had enough of their day-long nap and began circling a ceramic bowl in the kitchen. Maggie stood and placed the letter on the wooden kitchen table. She turned her back towards it and filled the ceramic bowl with kibbles. Once they had their fill of dinner, she scooped up a cat in each arm and headed to bed. With a chair lodged against her bedroom door handle, she crawled into bed and left the lamp on.

Maggie woke the next morning to Darcy purring in her ear. She stretched and, for a moment, all was right in the world. She walked into the kitchen to make breakfast for everyone and pretended not to see the letter. She casually placed a dish rag over the envelope as she cleaned up the kitchen.

It was evening before Maggie made it back around to the row of mailboxes by the homestead. She left this part of the route for last. The sun was just starting to dip below the distant mountains when she looked over at the gate.

The skeleton was gone.

She finished the row of mailboxes, and nothing was in the homestead box. She sat there and stared at the gate, then scanned the entire property and surrounding fields. There was nobody, no skeleton. She got out of the truck and slowly walked down the path but stopped a few feet away from the gate. She squinted her eyes to focus as the sun was starting to fade. There appeared to be another yellowed envelope attached to the gate. She looked around and then hurried the last few steps to the gate and grabbed the envelope. She didn't need to read the name on the front. She knew it was for her.

When she arrived home, she sat at the kitchen table and stared between the new envelope and the dish rag. She set the envelope down and slowly lifted the rag. There was nothing underneath it. She peeked under the table and along the floor. The original envelope was gone. She looked back at the new envelope, and it was then that she noticed the small tear on the side, the one she had made the night before.

The next day she called in sick.

On Friday, her boss called and asked her to please come in as they had a party planned for her. She made a few attempts at a feeble cough and said she was too sick to do her route. He promised that she would not have to deliver mail, just come to the party. She finally agreed and hid the letter under the sofa pillow before she left.

A few co-workers came and went, wishing her the best in retirement. They asked her what she planned to do now. She didn't really have an answer and just shared stories of spending time with her cats and reading the stack of books waiting by her nightstand. She finished the day in good spirits and enjoyed all the attention, even though most were just there for the cake.

As she was heading to her car, Nancy, the sweet front desk girl, ran up to her with a flower box filled with long-stemmed white and black roses. "Maggie, these were just delivered for you." The young woman handed her the box, gave one final hug, and left.

Maggie set the box down on the hood of her car and opened

the clear lid. She rubbed the smooth petals and breathed in the aroma.

Who sent them?

She dug underneath the roses and pulled out an envelope. It was yellowed with age and again, a small tear on the side. She left the roses on the hood of her car, sat down in the driver's seat, and shut and locked the doors. She peered out all the windows, half expecting the skeleton to be watching her. No one was in the parking lot, no witnesses. She ripped open the envelope, and inside was a letter and the postcard. The letter was written in the same heavy yet elegant black ink as her name on the front.

Dear Margaret Allred,

Congratulations on your retirement! A celebration will occur on Friday, September 28, in your honor. The festivities will begin at 8:00 p.m. Please RSVP if you will be attending.

Sincerely,

Harold Krum

Maggie folded the letter and then looked at the postcard. It was the same one she had seen before, a picture of the homestead on the front and one line on the back. Today was the 28th. It didn't give her much time to decide. Maybe this was a joke, a joke that had been building for thirty years. It couldn't be her old boss as he died a few years back. She hadn't told anyone else about the skeleton or the postcards. Maggie backed out of the parking spot as the box of roses fell off the hood of her car and onto the ground. She drove towards the homestead.

She pulled straight up to the last mailbox and then stared at the gate. No skeleton. It was actually more unsettling to not see him after all these years. She looked down at the post card, circled the yes, and placed it in the mailbox.

That night she paced around her one-bedroom house,

wearing a path through every room. Several times she tried talking herself out of going.

What if something bad happens? Who would take care of my cats? She paused for a moment—*who would miss me?*

She had never married or had children. She only had a few friends in the neighborhood that she waved to on occasion or who brought her sweet treats around the holidays. She never really felt as part of a group. She mainly kept to herself and found comfort in her cats. It could be days or weeks before someone noticed she was gone.

Around 7:00 p.m., she stared at her closet.

What do you wear to a party with a skeleton in the middle of an empty field?

The invitation didn't state a dress code. She finally settled on a pair of black slacks and a yellow sweater. She thought the bright yellow would be noticeable from the road if there was trouble.

Trouble? Should I remind you that you're insane for seriously considering going? What is wrong with you?

Maggie ignored her inner shouting and put on a pair of good winter boots. It was getting colder, and the ground would be misty. She hated for her toes to get cold. She watered the plants, then put the cats and a full bowl of kibbles on the front porch. Darcy and Sassy stared at the new surroundings with displeasure and rubbed up against the front door. Maggie picked up each and gently kissed them on the nose.

At 7:50 p.m., Maggie's car cleared the hill overlooking the homestead. She hit the brakes abruptly and stopped in the middle of the road. The lot was no longer empty. There stood the homestead, in its prime with bright lights shining through every window. It was like a beacon calling to her.

Maggie continued down the road, turned into the driveway, and drove through the now open gate, straight up to the steps leading to the front porch. As she stepped out of the car, she could hear laughter and band music coming from inside the home. Nervousness was quickly overtaken by joy and excitement as to what was about to happen. She walked up the front porch stairs and knocked on the front door.

Nobody answered.

She looked toward the side windows and could see silhouettes of people walking past them in the folds of the thin curtains. She thought maybe the music was too loud, and they couldn't hear her knock. She finally turned the knob, opened the door, and walked into a large entryway. Warm air filled her lungs with a delicious mixture of pumpkin pie and warm bread. She remembered the aromas from her childhood, standing in grandma's kitchen during the holidays. Her fears were erased as she embraced the warmth throughout her mind, body, and soul.

She looked around, and there was nobody to greet her. All the lights were on as she peeked into each room. They were empty. Not a stick of furniture. Smooth wooden floors with not a smudge or track. Where were the music and laughter coming from?

Everyone must be upstairs.

A wide staircase rose before her to the second level. She eagerly walked up the steps and took the path to the left. It curved back towards another smaller stairwell that led to the attic and the large balcony overlooking the front lawn. She saw a light at the top of the stairs and heard footsteps above her. She giggled as she embraced another scent from long ago, her father's aftershave. She would always climb in his lap and rub her cheek against his after he would shave. She would carry his scent upon her cheek throughout the day. He always made her feel safe and loved.

She climbed to the top of the stairs and paused. The attic was pitch black except for light pouring out around the closed double doors leading to the balcony. The aromas grew heavier, and the music louder with every step towards the balcony. She grabbed both of the smooth copper knobs and pulled open the double doors. A blinding light warmed her smiling face. She was overcome by a wave of love and belonging she had so long forgotten and desired. She was finally home.

Maggie walked out onto the balcony to a roar of welcoming cheers. The doors closed behind her with a rush of dead silence and blackness.

AROUND 1:00 A.M., the phone rang. A man who had been in deep sleep reached for his cell phone.

"Blakeman," grumbled the man.

"Sir, there's been another death at the homestead," said the voice on the phone.

Detective Blakeman didn't say a word, only hung up the call and stared into the darkness. He had been working homicide for almost twenty-five years and had investigated several deaths at the old homestead. He already knew what he would find. The broken body of an older man or woman as though they had jumped to their death. There would be no next of kin to notify. The politicians would want to keep the story from leaking. People were just starting to forget the old place, and a new death would stir up the crazies again.

The first couple of deaths were thought to be suicides, as it appeared they had jumped from the balcony of the old homestead. That was why the city burned the house down. Unfortunately, that didn't stop the deaths.

How could someone jump to their death in the middle of an empty lot?

He was hoping to finish out the last few years of his career without another incident at the homestead. He tried to accept that he would never be able to solve the mystery. There were only two bits of evidence that tied all the deaths. The first was a postcard found near the bodies. The second was a skeleton—in a damn bowler hat, no less. Always standing in the distance, watching. No one else seemed to notice him and Blakeman never mentioned the skeleton in his reports. Who would believe him?

THAT NEW CAR SMELL

LEO KEITH

Dramatic Short Story

*J*t's Friday evening, and I'm holding Deb's hand as we drive down the freeway. On a whim, and after a quick long-distance phone call, we arranged to visit her parents for the weekend. I'm driving my old car, which I'd bought from my uncle. In the few months I'd had it, I'd only made one significant change. I replaced his 8-track with a new cassette tape player.

I met Deb in our junior year at college and tied the knot shortly after our graduation. It takes us several hours when we travel to see our families, her parents to the north and mine to the west. It's far enough away to make our visits possible but not easy.

As we pull into the driveway, I hear Deb softly say, "Not again."

The garage door was up, and I see an unfamiliar sedan.

"At least this time," she says, "he was thinking of Mom." I listen as Deb explains her father's tendency to buy a new car every three or four years. His last purchase, still in the driveway, was a pickup.

As soon as we're in the door, Dean starts to tell me about all the bells and whistles. He promises that tomorrow after Barbara makes breakfast, we'll all take a drive out through the farmland, so he can show off his new prize.

Our Saturday includes waffles and sausage, Dean's promised ride, and a shopping trip to the mall. During dinner, Deb's kid sister Teresa tells us about the latest James Bond movie. My wife gets excited, and before I know it, we're planning to catch the late showing. "James, Debra, please take my car," Dean volunteers with a grin, excited to share his new pride and joy.

"DEBBIE?" I hear as we enter the theater. "I could have guessed if I saw you, it would be at a Bond show."

I feel Deb's grip on my hand tighten. As we turn, I see a fellow about my age, slightly smaller, wearing a theater uniform. His brown hair is pulled back.

"Hi, Steve," Deb says. "I'd like you to meet my husband, James."

Suddenly, I don't want to let go of Deb's hand. As I look over this stranger, his gaunt, weasely appearance sets my stomach to churning.

"How's it going with Jeanette?" Deb asks, her voice just a notch higher than usual.

"It didn't last," Steve starts, but he leaves the thought hanging. The distant look in his eyes tells me he expects Deb to understand.

"Oh, sorry to hear that."

Soon, Deb relaxes her tone and her hand in mine. Their conversation is more casual. I listen as they ask each other about friends and family. Some I know of, most I don't. Sometimes Steve's answers are detailed, and others only tell the city where they were living.

"I heard about Scott," she says softly. The conversation is slowing down. "I'm sorry."

Steve looks down at the floor again. "It could have been me."

My jaw tightens as Deb releases my hand, stepping towards this other man. I've only just met him and already have a dislike. My body tenses, an unsolicited gut reaction, like a fight is coming as Deb gives Steve a hug. I feel the adrenalin rise the longer their embrace lasts.

"Goodbye," she finally says softly. Only then do they separate.

Steve doesn't say a thing, just holds a somber gaze on Deb's face.

I'm about to burst when she plants a kiss on his cheek.

My lips are pursed as we find our seats. I have a pain in my chest when I think of Deb giving that embrace. It's not just that they hugged or that it appeared so natural. It was too long.

"So, who was he?" I finally ask as the Bond theme music starts.

"An old boyfriend," she answers as she looks over her shoulder. "We dated for over a year."

I try to not look at her. I want to be understanding, but I want to know more. I want her to tell me, to offer it to me. Just as she offered that hug.

They dated for over a year? Why am I learning this just now? And when will she tell me more? My mind is spinning as I imagine that hug from every angle. And who else knows about Steve? If Deb doesn't say, can I get insights from her family? Maybe Teresa will volunteer something tomorrow. Isn't that what kid sisters do? Maybe. Hopefully.

I'm holding Deb's hand, and my eyes are on the screen. My heart is pounding, and my mind is back in the lobby.

I ALLOW myself to get caught up in the movie until the closing credits start to roll. As if on cue, the image of Deb hugging Steve comes back to my mind. As we walk through the lobby, my eyes focus on where the offending embrace happened. I'm hoping that she'll open up any moment, reassure me that there was never anything between her and Steve.

What I really want is a hug, long enough to convince me that there's no one else but me.

She still hasn't said a word or made a move when we get to Dean's car.

"Dammit, slow down," she exclaims as I drive through the parking lot. I pretend wordlessly that I'm enjoying Dean's car with the aroma of the new molding around me. I doubt she believes it and repeats herself as I pull onto the street.

I don't say a word, wanting her to feel the sting I felt as I watched her holding another man. And I know it isn't rational.

Still, I tell her I need to get to bed early because of the drive home tomorrow.

Once in the guestroom, I can hear Deb talking to her mother. All I catch are a few names, Steve and Scott the most frequent.

And mine.

I FINALLY WAKE UP MID-MORNING. I stay in bed long enough to make sure Deb is still asleep, then slip down the hall. I've spent enough time with Deb's family to know Sunday breakfasts come from the cereal box, not the waffle iron. I decide on Lucky Charms, grab the milk, and sit at the table. Soon, Teresa helps herself to a bowl of cereal and starts talking about the movie. I realize this is my chance. If I'm careful, my sister-in-law will tell me what I need to know about Steve.

After a couple of minutes of exchanging details of villains and Bond's gadgets, I change the subject. "We met an old friend of Deb's at the theater last night."

"Oh, anyone I would know?" she asks as she reloads her spoon.

"His name is Steve," I say, but it feels colder than I'd intended. I turn to watch.

Her mouth is open wide, ready to accept the cereal frozen inches from her lips. Slowly, she puts the bite of breakfast in her mouth and starts to slowly chew. All the while, her eyes are locked on the sink opposite the table.

"I've got to hurry," she says quickly, "or I'll be late for church." Before I can say a word, she's grabbed her almost-empty dish and leaves. And I know she doesn't like church.

My shoulders slump, and my heart drops. Teresa had been my one hope of some insights. Barbara is the emotional backbone of the family. If Deb hasn't told me yet, my mother-in-law won't be the first to give me the news.

I finish my cereal and put things away. I look for Dean and find him listening to a Sunday news program while sorting through papers in his den. My inquiry to him gives me details appropriate to a family sitcom storyline. I hear about Steve's family, the basics of a few dates he had with Deb, and other light details. The one thing Dean says, adding perspective, is that, "Deb was heartbroken when she broke up with him. But she needed to do it." I switch topics, and soon, Dean and I are talking about the motor size and other details of his sedan.

After a while, I hear footsteps behind me. Barbara says, "We're leaving for church," as Teresa and Deb pass by. My wife and I have an agreement about religion. She won't push it, and I won't object to her going.

I thank Dean for the information, excuse myself from the den, and soon find Barbara's bookshelf in the family room to help pass the time. I find a wide variety of books, ranging from sci-fi novels to self-help books, peppered with historical biographies. I start by browsing through an old paperback, *Dennis the Menace: Household Hurricane.*

As I flip through the pages, my mind bounces between what happened last night, what I want to learn, and what I think will happen. In my gut, I know that Deb will be able to explain everything. My heart keeps dragging me back to last night, replaying that hug. More than ever, I want to smash Steve's face.

When Deb returns from church, there are two more in the car. I recognize her friends from our wedding line. My heart sinks, and I know I won't get anything important before we leave for home.

HOURS HAVE PASSED as we rumble down the freeway, and we still aren't talking. The radio is off since we can't agree on what to listen to. Her case of mix tapes is open between us. My stinky old car starts to shimmy, reminding me of Dean's sedan and the smooth ride.

"You're not being fair," she finally says softly.

I know. I just don't want to admit it.

"I knew Steve since junior high when he moved into the neighborhood." Her voice was firm and measured. "All his friends were my friends."

"Including Scott?" I ask.

"Scott and Steve were cousins," she answered. "We were in high school when Scott came for a summer visit, and he'd changed. That's when Steve started hanging around with people I didn't like. He's the reason I broke up with Steve."

The silence settles in again as I focus on passing a semi-truck.

"James," she says, looking out the window. "That's a part of my life I want to forget." There was a long pause. "I should have broken up with Steve long before I did. Before I ended up in the hospital."

The empty pit in my stomach tells me I need to be quiet and listen.

"I don't know if I was an addict," she says somberly. "I know I didn't like what I saw in the mirror in the hospital room. I didn't recognize myself. When I heard Scott say my name last night, my first thought was that he wanted me to use." She turns and looks at me, and I see her face, tight as she fails to contain her sobs. With her tears flowing freely, she continues, "If you hadn't been holding my hand, I might have. I wanted to."

The rest of our trip is a long, hard conversation as Deb explains things she needs to say, things I need to understand.

"Why didn't you tell me about this before?" I ask softly as we pass the sign for the state line. We'll be home soon.

"Some of my close friends said I should tell you before we married," she says. "Others said you didn't ever need to know. Mom said I'd know when the right time would be. She said that again last night."

We make the rest of the ride in silence, our fingers lightly laced together. I want to say something, but the right words aren't forming in my mind. I'll have to do more than just apologize for being a jealous jerk.

As we park in front of our apartment, I'm finally able to turn and look, undistracted, into my wife's eyes. Her lips are pursed, her eyebrows a little high. Her eyes are red, still soft with tears. "Please understand," she says. "It wasn't just because you were with me at the theater. It's because you are with me. Always."

I release her hand, move mine up behind her neck, and pull her gently towards me. First, our foreheads press together, then our cheeks before I give her a light, reassuring kiss. She returns it, long and tender.

I search long and deep for the right words to say, some way to let her know I understand, or at least want to. "Thanks," is the best I can come up with. For now, it will have to do. It's then I know that we have ways that we need to grow, both together.

"We need to unpack," she says. "Work will come early for both of us."

Once in our bedroom, her mood lightens. She starts to tell me about a time she pranked her father. "While he was at work, we swapped his new Buick with a beat-up Ford we borrowed from a used car lot."

I assume her partner was Steve, but I don't ask.

She's grinning as she throws my other pair of pants at me. I'm distracted by the subtle thump I feel. I have something in the pocket that shouldn't be there.

Her eyes are wide, her hand to her mouth as she suppresses a giggle. In my hand, I hold the key to Dean's new car.

"Do you think our budget can afford another long-distance call?" I ask with a smile. "We'll get the weekend rate."

With a deep breath, I wait as Deb punches in her parent's phone number. Once it starts to ring, she hands me the receiver. All I can think is that I'm grateful Dean has welcomed me into the family.

After a quick hello and reporting our safe arrival, I confess. "Dean, I've got the key to your car."

"Well, that explains why I can't find it," he says. "Drop it in the mail when you get a chance. It's a new car, and I've got a spare."

I hadn't even thought of that.

"James, put Debra on," Dean says. "Barbara wants to talk to her."

I hand Deb the phone as I step into the bedroom. I can still hear her side of the conversation. "Yes, we talked. Yes, he knows. No, we only had a few hours. I haven't told him everything, yet."

I try to ignore the call, with mixed success. I distract myself by thinking of our talk, the ride home, and Dean's car.

After a few minutes, Deb comes in. She hooks her arms around my neck and pulls me into a hug. "Thanks," she says. "And Mom says thanks, too. She also says you're a good man."

We hold the hug for a long time. I finally break the silence. "How about I pick you up after work? There's something I want to do for you. It's been on my mind since since we drove away."

Deb looks up at me, her eyes wide with excitement. "That new car smell?"

I CHANGED ME

VIRGINIA BABCOCK

Contemporary Romance

On her daily trek to the mailbox, Isla halted, feeling deep vibrations in the ground under her feet. She covered her ears with her hands and scrunched her eyes tightly closed as the truck drove by. Gritting her teeth barely enabled her to control her temper. Why did so many heavy dirt hauler semis have to blow by the house before breakfast? When the last wheel passed, she sneezed in the dusty air.

She had grown to detest living here. Her great-aunt's house used to be surrounded by hay fields and horse pastures. But a massive developer had bought the farm across the way, and voila, the family's ten-acre home farm was surrounded by the landscaped yards of mini-mansions. Now, the developer was doing something with the old gravel pit that had devoured the foothills. Even if they hadn't received a flyer, Isla would have known something was up by the amount of heavy truck traffic.

She deposited her great aunt's latest round of letters in the heavy, antique tin mailbox and raised the flag. Every few days, her aunt's circle from the older generation would exchange letters.

Since the pandemic had moved the octogenarians to isolate, they'd used cell phones and pen pal letters to stay connected. Ironically, only a few talked on the phones. Most texted, sending pictures back and forth. The conversations were in letters, and they'd formed chain letters to conference as groups. Written communication well suited most of the group's slow days and individual timetables.

Making the trip out to the mailbox morning and night gave her aunt a reason to move around now that the livestock was gone. However, she'd stepped wrong and wrenched her ankle, making letter delivery and retrieval Isla's duty for the next few days.

More rumbles heralded another truck, this one empty and barreling in the other direction. Isla closed her eyes again. It honked loudly and braked hard, making a complete stop before quickly roaring away. She blinked and looked around. There at the corner of the yard, the bushes in the hedge bordering the curb shook, raising a small dust cloud. Isla walked closer. On the roadside of the hedge, something furry was frantically struggling. She spotted a black tail, the width and length of her pinkie finger.

Isla checked the road before stepping over the low foliage onto the street. Skid marks on the pavement and a residual burnt rubber smell confirmed the truck had paused there. She noticed a line of baling twine tied around the nearby sprinkler head that stood sentinel at the edge of the lawn. The twine ran tautly along the cement curb and disappeared under the foliage. She grabbed it and tugged. Yipping accompanied a tiny black pup as she dragged it backward.

The plastic twine was tied around the baby dog's neck. "Poor little thing." Compassion for the pup swamped Isla. She released the pressure on the cord as she reached for the pup. She didn't want to choke it. Miniature claws and barely weaned milk teeth nipped at her fingers and hands. In distress, the puppy peed a little on her as she lifted it out from amongst the roots. It was a short-haired breed and male. It shivered and whined in her arms.

Isla noticed a half-circle in the dirt arcing out on the asphalt. The scuff marks showed the puppy had been battling against his tether for a while.

Thankfully, the orange twine was knotted in a way to keep the loop from tightening and strangling the pup. Isla gritted her teeth in frustration. There was no give to the plastic fibers, and she didn't have a knife handy. Shifting the pup to one arm, she went to work on the knot. The puppy squirmed and wiggled, but she finally got a fingernail under one of the loops. Concentrating, she pulled it loose and flung the twine end away. A loud honk sounded again.

Isla hurriedly stepped across the bushes and carried the puppy around the back into the house. He was still shaking with fear and nuzzling against her. He couldn't be more than a few weeks old. At the kitchen sink, she filled a small saucer with water and snagged a biscuit she'd baked yesterday from the cookie jar. She set the puppy on the counter and held her hand on it as it drank.

Aunt Leona's friend owned a health food store and kept them stocked in "teething" biscuits via crates of frozen dough balls. Leona's teeth were sound, but the chemo fighting the cancer eating through her skin had destroyed her appetite. These hard but appetizing, easily digestible, and delicious cookies were satisfying and nutrient-rich for babies and those with small appetites. If needed, Leona could make it through a day on these biscuits and the sweet ginger tea she drank constantly.

The biscuits smelled like their ingredients: roasted oats, ginger, and honey, and didn't put Leona off her chow. She woke up nauseous and cranky most days. Isla had been using the scrumptious baking smells of the biscuits to entice Leona into the kitchen to eat each morning.

Isla checked the clock. The puppy was putting her behind schedule. She snagged another day-old cookie, crumbled off a small bit, and held it under the puppy's nose. It sniffed and then licked at the crumbs and her fingers. Sloppily, it gobbled down the biscuit and half another in teeny bites. Then it paused and peed.

Isla gasped and yanked the puppy down to the floor. Thankfully, the paper towels were close. She swiped a handful down the counter and sopped up the mess on the floor. She left the puppy wandering the kitchen's vinyl floor as she started a sink of hot soapy water and ducked into the pantry for the cleaning caddy.

By the time Isla finished cleaning, Leona had lumbered lopsidedly into the kitchen and carefully sat at the table. Isla was dressed in clean clothes, had stashed the sleeping puppy in a box on the screened-in back porch, and had a heaping plate of hot cookies on the pristine and sanitized counter.

They ate breakfast in a companionable way and enjoyed the sunny morning, sipping tea and munching on cookies for the hour it took Leona to wake up and go through her phone messages. Today's plan was to lounge in the front room with Leona reading and writing letters while intermittently watching TV as Isla worked on her laptop.

When she could spare a few minutes, Isla unobtrusively checked on the pup. It slept most of the day. As her aunt snoozed on the couch for her typical afternoon nap, Isla scooped up the used newspaper and dirty towel from the puppy's box and replaced them. The puppy followed her around, so she held the screen door open to let it follow her outside. Isla deposited the used newsprint in the massive trash bag where she'd stashed the dirty paper towels earlier. Hopefully, getting the trash out quickly would keep the doggish smells far away from Leona's nose.

The puppy trailed her into the shop, where she dropped the towel into the washing machine on top of her outfit and the cleaning rags from earlier, and started the load. This washer and dryer were a duplicate set her uncle installed out here to handle the nasty laundry loads that were inevitable when working on a farm. Isla hoped Leona not seeing the extra laundry would help keep the puppy's presence a secret until she knew they could keep him.

She was heading back into the house when Isla heard a vehicle stop out front and a car door shut. She sprinted around the side of the house and successfully intercepted the visitor on the front porch before they could ring the doorbell and wake Leona.

The young man saw her and turned, carrying a vase full of blooming lilac branches. He asked, "Are you Isla Overton?"

"Yes."

"Good. These are for you."

Isla adjusted her hold on the heavy glass vase as the delivery man got back into the florist's van and drove off.

"Isla! What's that?" Her aunt's voice boomed from the front porch.

Isla turned to face her. "Flowers."

Leona shook her head. "No, that." She pointed to Isla's legs.

Isla looked down. The puppy had followed her and was sniffing around her ankles. Resigned, she faced her aunt's angry face. "A puppy."

"I can see that. Where did it come from?"

"Someone tied him to your sprinkler sometime yesterday or last night. I found him this morning."

"This morning?" Aunt Leona threw up her hands and headed back into the house.

Gingerly, Isla squatted and scooped up the puppy without

tipping the blossoms.

At the kitchen table, the women negotiated the puppy's future. Leona handled him and pronounced him not a Rottweiler or Doberman despite his tan points, eyebrows, and paws. "The skull and nose are too narrow. He looks like our Border Collie pups. But all breeds' puppies look the same at this age." Leona cradled the yawning puppy against her arm. "Everyone knows Shep passed on last month. I wonder if someone gifted us a new dog."

Seeing Aunt Leona hold the sleeping pup calmed Isla's worries. She'd been hoping to get a new dog. Aunt Leona had hinted that Shep was her last dog, ever. Isla prayed the puppy would give her aunt something positive to look forward to each day.

"So, the lilacs. Who are they from?" Leona asked.

Isla looked through the flowers. Her fingers brushed something tied to the ribbon around the vase. She pulled the tiny card out of the florist's envelope and read out: "Isla, please come to the town hall tonight."

Leona's brows raised. "The developer's town hall meeting tonight about the quarry?"

"It must be. They put flyers all over the neighborhood."

"But don't you have that dinner?"

"Yes. And I can't miss my boss's birthday party. I'm in charge of the games."

"Well, that's fine. The person sending you the flowers should have asked you in person or on the phone."

THE PUPPY WHINING WOKE Isla from a sound sleep. Concern for the state of the floors got her moving to the box and depositing the puppy on the back yard's grass post haste. She yawned widely and took a deep breath of the brisk morning air. She moved to the side of the house to look at the mountains. The sky was pink, but the rising sun hadn't yet breached their heights.

The rumblings of two loaded semi earth haulers going by drew her attention. Their dust clouds had just settled when a tiny, white car pulled up. Isla intercepted the driver as they stepped onto the front walk.

The delivery woman held a box marked with a food delivery service logo. "You Isla Overton?"

"Yes."

The woman handed over the box. "These are for you." She returned to her car.

Isla called out, "Who is it from?"

The driver answered over her shoulder, "Don't know. The receipt should have a message."

A little later, when Leona entered the kitchen, Isla was baking more cookies. The puppy lay sideways on the floor nearby, chewing on a bit of rawhide. Leona looked at the box and saw a bowl of oranges on the table. "Another delivery?"

Isla nodded. "Yes. This one read, 'Sorry to miss you last night. Be home tonight, please.'"

"So, your admirer is determined."

"Seems like."

"Is there something you're not telling me? After the dust-up with Rolf all those years ago, have you met someone new?"

Isla covered her eyes with her hand. "No. I haven't dated anyone seriously in a long time. Damn. I haven't thought of Rolf in a while." Dread filled her. She studiously avoided talking about Rolf. Sadness, guilt, and regret were all she had left from that relationship.

Leona noticed Isla's hesitation. "Oh, honey. I'm sorry. I didn't mean to upset you." Leona moved over and enveloped Isla in a hug. After a moment, Leona urged Isla to sit at the table.

"Thanks, Auntie. I'm just sensitive. I made so many mistakes with Rolf. I don't know why he put up with me as long as he did."

"You two did grow up together. What happened?"

"I'm sure Mom and Gran filled you in on all the details."

"No, actually, they didn't. Your mom didn't tell me anything. Nan only told me you two broke up during college. I knew you were no longer an item when he came home from school, but I thought you matched each other perfectly, especially on that prom night when you came here to let Justin and me feed you."

"That was a great night." Isla shook her head. "It's not a happy tale, and anyone will tell you I was the villain."

"So, what happened?"

"Too much, really. We dated throughout most of high school. Half of sophomore year and all of junior year. Then in senior year, he took that trip to Germany. We fought and, out of revenge, I dated someone else while he was gone. We broke up as soon as Rolf found out. I thought that was the end. Maybe it should have been." Recriminations ran through Isla's thoughts. "At college, did Gran mention my grades?"

"No. Only that you took a while to get done. I figured money got tight, and you pared down your schedule."

"Rolf and I reconnected in college during our freshman year, and things went well until the start of sophomore year. The classwork was harder and stressed me out, and I started fighting with Rolf fairly frequently. Then for my twenty-first birthday, my roommates took me to Vegas. He didn't want me to go. A bunch of us got drunk—me for the first time that weekend. Later on, when school got really hard or I needed a break, I started partying more and harder. I began drinking regularly. Rolf agreed to be my DD at first but tired of my behavior soon enough. I kept partying without him and was drunk nearly every weekend. I began drinking every day and started missing classes. When I did go, after class, I'd drop my bag on the counter and pick up a bottle. At my peak, I was drinking a fifth of tequila each day. I started in the afternoon and drank until I passed out."

"Was this around the time Justin took you to St. George?"

"Yes. Mom called him for help. Rolf had told her all about me. She and Rolf had tried to do an intervention, during which I stormed out. Mom begged Uncle Justin to get me to rehab."

"Oh. How did that go?"

"Driving across the state with Uncle Justin was better than expected. I was hungover and suffering withdrawals, but he told me the family secret, which made me feel better."

Leona confirmed, "He told you that my mother, your great grandmother, was a lush and that this God-fearing family has spawned secret drunks for generations?"

"That's it. Mom has always stayed staunchly on the temperance side and obsessively avoided any alcohol, so she was naturally horrified by my behavior. She hid me away from everyone who knew me 'before.' She went totally ballistic when the facility gave her my medical report. Chlamydia. She didn't like learning I was a sexy drunk and had contracted an STD. She cut me off. That's still in effect, by the way. I can never live under her roof again. Thank you, as always, for giving me a place to stay."

Leona patted Isla's hand. "Nan told me you were *persona non grata* with your mother. But you and I have always got along." She looked deeply into Isla's eyes. "You don't seem to have those problems now?"

"That's because I am a 'recovered' alcoholic. I've been sober for five years. I had to redo college entirely, even the classes I passed. I couldn't remember what I'd learned. Dad continues to complain that I cost him two college educations. I also cost him thousands of dollars for rehab. It's possible that my strain on the family finances caused their divorce. Another reason Mom disowned me."

Isla paused for a hiccup. "There's more. The reason I can't get my own place is that I have $5,000 left to pay on a judgment that's blackened my credit for nearly a decade. Not only did Rolf and I break up for good after he found me in bed with his roommate, which to this day I do not remember, but there are pictures; I wrapped his truck around a cop's oak tree. I nearly ran over my best friend's dad with Mom's car. I lost my license, my car, my respect. Finally, I had an abortion. I can't fix anything I broke and can never repay all those I hurt, but some have forgiven me." Isla's eyes filled with tears. "I understand if you want me to leave."

Leona hugged her again. Against Isla's cheek, she said, "In the eighteen months you've lived here, you've been nothing but a godsend to this old widow. I love you, honey."

"Love you, too, Auntie. I worried about the puppy, but I was certain you'd kick out a drunk."

Leona shook her head and smiled. "You silly one." She asked, "Those meetings every Thursday are AA?"

"Yes. And the odd phone calls … I'm a sponsor too."

"Well, I'm glad you made it through." Leona sat down. "That means the flowers aren't possibly from Rolf, and there's no new guy. Do you think you have an AA admirer?"

"I have no idea." Isla gulped down the bile that had risen in her throat. "About the abortion … I didn't want to end the pregnancy, but had no idea who the father was, and everyone was sure the baby would have Fetal Alcohol Syndrome." Tears spilled out of Isla's eyes. "Nightmares showing a tiny baby girl, stillborn with the flat lip and small eyes of a FAS baby were the trigger that made me accept treatment. Although, Rolf's frowning face got me close. Have you ever seen someone who loved you look at you with hate?"

Leona nodded. "Unfortunately, yes. But he forgave me, eventually. That doesn't always happen, does it?"

Isla chuckled sadly. "You're right about that."

Leona stood and hobbled to the cupboard. "Let's take today as it comes. I trust that the sender of the fruit and possibly the flowers will contact you tonight. Let's make brownies, but I'll also get the shotgun from the safe."

ISLA'S FINGERS flew over her work laptop's keyboard. She was surprised by how much better she felt after sharing her troubled past with her great aunt. It was like a load she didn't know she'd been lugging around was gone. The fact that Aunt Leona loved her regardless was amazingly comforting.

Leona looked up from her letter writing. "Oh, Isla, the mail just arrived, and a FedEx truck came by earlier. While you are getting the mail, please check for a package."

After handing the mail to Leona, Isla picked up the small, padded envelope addressed to her that had been stuck between the front and screen doors and opened it. A card and USB drive fell out. The card read, "Isla, please listen to the song. All will be explained."

Leona asked, "So?"

Isla handed her the card and plugged the drive into her computer. "It's supposed to be a song." She accessed a program. "Let me get work's security protocol going, in case this is a bad news drive, and then I'll play it."

The software deemed the drive safe and showed a single audio file: Crosby, Stills, and Nash's song, "Southern Cross." Isla clicked play.

Aunt Leona smiled. "Justin loved CSN, even when they were CSNY. That's the one Stephen Stills wrote after his divorce. It's about how the universe can help us heal and move on after we mess up."

Isla replayed the song and read the lyrics online. "I've heard it before too. I don't know anyone who would have this kind of connection to me."

Leona mused, "You ruled out Rolf, right? Anyone else from your past?"

Isla's mouth wrinkled to match her crunched-together eyebrows. "That's just it. There are whole years where I lived my life without remembering much of it. This could get messy."

Leona was pragmatic. She patted her pocket. "I've got the shotgun shells ready. If you'd rather show some mercy, I have the ones Justin filled with rock salt too." Her phone rang. She checked the screen and went into the kitchen to answer it.

Isla removed the drive and put it and the card back in the envelope. The thought that law enforcement may need to look at her mysterious deliveries floated through her mind.

Leona hollered, "Isla, the family who wants to board a horse here is coming by in twenty minutes. Can you get them settled?"

"Sure." Isla was grateful for a distraction. She fired off an email requesting the rest of the afternoon off. She darted upstairs to change into a pair of jeans and put on her boots. The puppy excitedly followed her. She took him outside and was playing in the grass with the pup when the clopping of metal-shod horse hooves on pavement sounded out front.

A gorgeous, dark bay draft horse was approaching, partially silhouetted by the setting sun. The rider was wearing a wide hat that shaded his face. Isla raised a hand. The rider waved in reply. Isla met them as they turned into the drive, greeting the horse with a carrot as she rubbed on the forehead along its white blaze. The puppy sniffed around the horse's front hooves as the man tapped his hat back higher on his forehead.

Isla recognized him as he greeted her.

"Hey, Isla."

"Hello, Rolf." A lightning-fast thought popped into Isla's head. *Aunt Leona knew he was coming and didn't say anything!*

Meanwhile, Rolf was looking down at her. "Meet Pepper.

Since her dam, Paprika died, she's been lonely. Dad wondered if we could board her here where she could be with other horses. At least until he gets a partner for her on the wagon. I heard the James's are boarding two here?"

"Uh, yes, they will be, starting next week." Unsure of how to proceed, Isla went for business-professional. "Join me at the pasture? It's just past the barn."

"Will do." He paused. "Can we talk after? Just for a few minutes?"

Isla nodded, quelling the urge to speculate on why he wanted to talk. She squatted, snagged the puppy into her arms, and led the way, her brisk pace easily matched by the huge horse.

At the barn abutting the largest pasture, Isla turned on the pump to fill the wide water trough that rested under the fence, half in and out of the pasture. Rolf stopped Pepper nearby. He dismounted using the fence rails and led Pepper to the trough, where she drank thirstily.

Isla opened the barn's big door and retrieved a brush from the tack room. She tried *not* to think about how well Rolf looked riding a draft horse that would dwarf a smaller person. Manly seemed too weak a word to describe his large, tall, well-muscled physique.

Rolf tethered Pepper to the gate and flipped up the stirrup so he could unbuckle the saddle's cinch strap.

Isla stood at Pepper's head. "The saddle stand is ready. You okay leaving the tack here?"

Rolf turned his head to look at her. "Yes, please. Mom would like to come by periodically to ride her."

"Sounds good. We leave the barn unlocked unless we're out of town. You bringing hay? Our fields are in corn this year instead of alfalfa."

"Dad is arranging for two one-ton bales tomorrow. Will that suit?"

"Absolutely. The hay barn is behind this one."

"I remember."

An important fact manifested within Isla's recall. For the two years she was in and out of rehab, he was here. "Oh. I forgot. You worked here for a while when Uncle Justin was sick." Isla swallowed her gorge and embarrassment. She'd tried to ignore Rolf working for her beloved aunt and uncle while she rebuilt her life. Ironically, she had actually forgotten.

"Yeah." Rolf turned to the horse.

They worked together without speaking. Rolf hefted the saddle. Isla carried the pad. While Rolf brushed Pepper's sweaty sides, Isla held her by the halter's heavy ring under her chin.

When he finished currying, Isla asked, "Halter off or on?"

"Oh, off. Pepper's well trained and loves Mom. She'll come right to her."

Isla noticed her forehead was still level with his chin. She quashed memories of how she used to rest her face against his neck.

Rolf opened the gate and hung back as Isla led Pepper into the pasture, the horse's head dipping immediately to nab some fresh clover. Isla worked to undo the halter, then handed it with the lead rope to Rolf. The puppy followed them into the pasture. Isla picked him up and closed the gate as Rolf stashed the remaining tack in the barn.

He closed the barn door and ambled closer. When he stood toe to toe with her, he scratched the puppy's head. "Cute pup. What's its name?"

"To be determined. We only got him yesterday."

"Mom told me Shep passed. He was the last dog Justin trained, right?"

"Yep. Definitely the end of an era." Isla ran out of things to say.

Rolf was silent too.

She looked at him.

He raised an eyebrow.

She sighed. "So, you wanted to talk?"

"Yes. But can we sit in the kitchen? It's still hot out, and I used to talk for hours at that table with your great aunt and uncle."

Isla's first instinct was to decline. A memory of Uncle Justin clasping Rolf's shoulders made her reconsider. Belatedly, she recognized the formality of his request. Justin always held his most serious conversations in the kitchen. "Uh, sure. Follow me, I guess."

They met Leona standing in the kitchen munching on a biscuit as the electric kettle heated water for tea.

Leona's face lit up. "Rolf, when your mom said someone was bringing the horse over, I didn't expect you. It's good to see you, though. It's been a long time." She approached him and embraced him. "I heard you moved back to town, living in a monstrous house somewhere fancy."

Rolf hugged her back. "Once I made my so-called fortune, I did. Mom asked me to. And the house is actually just a house. I'd like to show it off to you sometime."

"It's a date." Leona looked at Isla and then back to Rolf. Her kettle chimed. She handed the remainder of her biscuit to the puppy before filling her teapot waiting on its tray. She picked up the tray and turned to go to the living room. Over her shoulder, she said, "I suspect you two could use some privacy."

Rolf looked at Isla, pulled out a kitchen chair, and sat down. He motioned to the bowl of oranges. "These look good. Can I have one?"

"Sure." Isla grabbed two more biscuits for the pup and sat down across the table from him. The puppy nestled in her lap, nibbling as Rolf deftly peeled the orange.

Rolf nodded to the lilacs. "Those look nice. I wonder where they came from. Mom's were done by the end of April."

"I don't know. Someone sent them as a bouquet. The oranges too."

"Thank you for sharing."

They sat. Rolf ate his orange methodically, one section at a time. The puppy's contented growling and munching were the only sounds in the kitchen.

Irritation and confusion warred with curiosity making Isla prod, "So, you wanted to talk?"

Rolf set down his fruit. "Yes. First, you look great. It's been a while."

"Agreed. Ditto."

"I know the last time we spoke was ..." he paused.

The mental cord controlling Isla's temper started to fray. "Uncomfortable?" She cocked her head to one side.

He shook his head. "Actually, I would say traumatic, and maybe sad ... No ... tragic."

Isla felt tears well up, sadness neutralizing her anger. "Mom would say traumatic. She told everyone I didn't add drama to her life, but trauma."

Rolf reached a hand towards her. "Oh, Izzy."

She scowled.

He withdrew his hand.

A tear escaped Isla's eye, but her voice stayed firm. "You can't call me Izzy. You said you were done with me. You gave up that right that day."

"That's true. I'm sorry."

Another tear fell. She scrubbed it away.

Across the table, Rolf quietly muttered, "This is not how I planned things."

Isla choked out, "Planned what?"

Rolf nodded. "Can I level with you?"

"Please."

"It was me."

"What?"

"The dog, the lilacs, the oranges, the song. All me. I was trying to recreate a moment."

"What moment?"

Rolf breathed deep. "Don't you smell it? Close your eyes."

Isla obeyed him. The freshly peeled fruit amped up the orange fragrance, which added a tang to the sweet lilacs. She got a whiff of ginger and oats from the tea and biscuits, and just a hint of dog. She focused on the lilac's odor and then the orange's. Suddenly, she remembered. Her eyes popped open. "The sheep camp?"

Rolf nodded.

Isla wondered at the glistening in his eyes.

His voice was thick, "The best day we had."

"The last good day we had." Isla shook her head. "Why? Why now? Why me?"

"Because I couldn't wait any longer. Because I've spent years trying to find happiness, and I can't. Not without you."

"You weren't particularly happy *with* me."

"I bet you think that. I've heard some about what you've been doing for the past few years. I've been building a business empire and obsessing over how much wrong I did to the girl I loved."

"Hah. You said so yourself that I was the one at fault. I ruined your life as I was destroying mine."

"No. No!" Rolf ran his fingers through his hair. He stood up. "I was cocky and self-righteous. I took no credit for my bad acts and over-emphasized what I considered yours."

Isla shook her head at him.

He shot back at her. "It's true! You developed a habit ..."

"An addiction."

"Fine, you were an addict, an alcoholic, whatever. I was a dick. I talked you into sex at fifteen before you were really ready. I abandoned you our senior year in high school to get college credit and see Germany. I threw a hissy fit when your girlfriends wanted to treat you to a birthday weekend in Vegas that I couldn't afford. And when you came back, I was so focused on what you were drinking that I totally missed that you were unhappy and had no idea of your struggles with some of your classes."

Isla was shocked.

Rolf sighed and continued, "Look. I planned to ask you for a new start. A do-over." He sat back down, dropping his face into his hands, his fingers rubbing his eyes. "I hoped the song would help."

AA's Step No. 9 popped into Isla's head. She could make some direct amends to Rolf right now. She applied some mercy to her feelings. "Rolf, what did you want the song to tell me?"

Rolf raised his head. His voice was flat, hopeless. "Figuratively, I have been around the world looking, but have never found the 'woman/girl' to replace the one I'd lost. And no other woman has ..." His voice cracked. He swallowed. "I can't forget loving you."

Isla's mouth dropped open. The lyrics he'd paraphrased reverberated in her head.

Rolf went on, "When my company got the contract to restore the quarry to a sustainable slope, I jumped at the chance to buy the adjoining farmland to develop. I built a showpiece on the best lot just over there," He pointed behind Isla "... and then realized I don't want to live there by myself. I drive by this place and see you and Leona and remember what we had. I wish I could get that back. I went so far as to ask Mom to find out if Leona wanted a new dog. That way, I could 'gift' you a puppy from Jackie's latest litter."

"Rolf, are you serious?" Isla paused. Rumblings from another big truck shook the house, distracting her. She pointed at him. "You're the reason I now live in the city? Those are *your* huge trucks thundering by all the time?"

Rolf looked taken back. "You mean I screwed up again? I

thought a new housing development here would help your aunt's property value increase. Without the livestock, I worried about her being able to pay her bills."

He looked to the ceiling. "For weeks, I've been remembering our last good day. A warm spring day in the mountains. Your family's lilacs in full bloom at the old homestead. Justin taking Leona out for a sit-down dinner on their anniversary, leaving us alone to babysit the sheep overnight. Me and you feasting on fresh oranges and fried chicken. Kicking Shep out of the Basque sheep camp wagon so we could make love undisturbed."

His voice broke, "I think about the car ride home the next day. You giggling that you snuck in and out a set of bedding, hoping they wouldn't know we'd had sex. You talked about the Vegas trip the coming weekend and plotted out some long-term plans for us."

Rolf reached into his shirt pocket and held up a solitaire ring. "Because I'd gotten so mad about the girls' weekend, I didn't give this to you that day. I'd planned to. Lately, I wonder how our lives would be if you'd gone to and returned from Vegas engaged. Maybe we would have moved into young married housing the next month. Maybe you would have had a supporting husband instead of a self-absorbed and insecure boyfriend."

Isla's halted tears returned in earnest, the noisy trucks forgotten. "I don't know what to say."

Rolf moved to her side, lifted her arm, and turned her wrist until her hand opened upward. He placed the ring in her palm. "I was hoping for a date after the meeting last night. Now, I think we have a few issues to address." His Adam's apple bobbed. "Please take this and keep it. I'll buy you a bigger one if you want." He closed her fingers over the ring. "I'd like to spend some time with you. I'm hoping we can try again, but do it better for longer this time. Can I come over tomorrow?"

The puppy yipped and started whining. Isla jumped out of the chair. "Oh. I need to get him outside."

Rolf plucked the puppy from her lap and headed out.

Isla followed him. When the puppy finished his business, he came over and laid against Isla's feet in the grass.

Rolf and Isla stared at each other.

Isla ventured, "I don't remember most of what I said or did when I was drinking. I'm sober and have been for years, but this disease will always be with me."

Rolf stood directly in front of her, careful of the puppy. "I've been a selfish, self-centered, spoiled SOB most of my life. I've been trying to turn that around, but you are the one thing I want, and I'm feeling more selfish than ever."

"We always want what we cannot have."

"I had you, and then I didn't. I want you back."

"You're sure?"

"I think so. At a minimum, I want a chance to start over with you. A chance to try 'us' again."

"I don't know …"

His grabbing her by the shoulders silenced her. He scrutinized her face.

For a moment, it felt weird and unfamiliar to be touched, held by him.

He spoke, "We haven't …"

She put up a hand. "No, we haven't touched in a very long time."

"I haven't held you since that day, have I?" He let go of her and stepped back.

"No, you stopped right before Vegas. We had that fight. After I got back, you held my hand a bit and kissed me a few times, but our last hug was as you dropped me off at the airport. We had sex a couple more times before we broke up, but you didn't hold me after like you used to."

He nodded, "You are right. I should have realized what I

wasn't doing. I am sorry." He looked sad. "Can we try, one time, just to see?" He held up his arms and took a step forward.

Isla met him. He placed his arms around her upper back. She placed hers around his waist. Isla shifted and twisted slightly until her chest was angled against his. She tilted her head until her cheek rested just below his collarbone. She breathed deeply and relaxed. Her actions seemed to prompt Rolf to also relax. He squeezed her lightly. His head lowered to rest on the top of hers.

He said, "I missed this. How are you doing?"

"I missed it too. You were a good friend to me."

He lifted his head and gently nudged her face up so he could look in her eyes. "Is that what you want from me now? Friendship?"

Isla ducked her face down. Against his chest, she answered, "I have enough friends. I do miss *your* friendship, but whenever anyone seriously asks me what I regret losing to alcoholism the most, I answer 'my love.' Love as in the love of my life. You were that love. The one I always wanted." She pulled away. Unable to raise her face, she stared at the grass without seeing it.

Rolf followed her and bent over her until his forehead was resting against the top of her head. "I wanted you for my wife. You were my one and only, too."

She lifted her face to his. Nose to nose they stood, waiting for her answer. When it came, it was very quiet. "I've dealt with the issues that I tried to solve with alcohol. I matured beyond the need to manipulate your feelings by dating other guys. But I haven't dated anyone seriously since you. I don't know what kind of partner, lover, or wife I can or would be. Are you willing to take that risk with me?"

Rolf answered after a few moments. "I've spent the past few minutes happier than I've been in years, probably since we split. I look at you, healed, competent, and settled, and joy fills my heart. Can I guarantee that you and I can be happy together?

No. Do I want to try? I think so. Why?" He reached for her hand and placed it palm-down on the center of his sternum. "Being with you makes me feel settled in my heart." He held his hand over hers. "You live here. Without you, I am half a person."

He backed away and released her hand.

Tears ran down Isla's cheeks unnoticed. She looked down at the puppy, up at the sky, over the yard and pastures, and then back to Rolf. She blinked a few times to clear the tears so she could see him. Tears marked his cheeks as well. She closed the distance between them. Her hands reached to his face, cupping his cheeks, thumbs wiping at the wetness there. She slid her fingers to the back of his neck and tugged his head down until his nose was a millimeter from hers. Her voice was fierce, and her eyes never left his as she vowed, "Never in a million years did I dream that you would ask me to love you again. But, if you are truly giving me a chance to have you for my very own, damn right I am going to take it. I loved you once, Rolf, and I can do so again."

His voice was hoarse. "Mean it?"

She nodded, unable to speak through the tightness in her throat.

AFTER ROLF HAD RETRIEVED his hat and left, Isla sat on the back steps, petting the puppy and staring into her future.

Leona appeared at the back porch door, the scent of lilacs accompanying her. "So?"

"It was Rolf. It was all Rolf." Isla looked up to her aunt. "He's coming again tomorrow."

"Good to hear. I'm glad it's someone I like. Your mom's new boyfriend is an ass."

MOVING BLUES

LEA GRAND

Contemporary Fiction

*O*ving day fast approached. Not even a fourth of my belongings in this old two-story house will fit in my new patio home. From my experiences as a military wife, moving didn't bother me. We lived light, never collecting much. But after my husband retired, our roots here have multiplied, strong and true. So has my 'stuff.'

With a sigh, I started in my bedroom. Not so much to decide what would have to go, but what I couldn't bear to lose. So much of my life was in the mementos. I stomped to my bureau to start at the top. Keep my jewelry; most was already listed as bequeaths in my will. Keep the antique hand-painted set of lidded bowls from my mother-in-law. A peek inside assured me one still held my collection of hat pins and the other the halflings, as I called all the earrings that had lost a partner, in hopes the other would turn up. As I reached for the little glass bowl that held the rings I wore every day, I knocked over a little bottle of perfume. Holding it up to the light, I saw it was almost empty. I smiled and lifted it over my head to give a soft spray. As the mist settled around me, it brought back the soft brown eyes of Michael, the military son I hadn't seen for far too long.

The Christmas he gave it to me was the first time he had his very own money, earned by dog walking. He was so proud as he babbled the story of my gift.

"I went into the department store downtown, the one you like," he said. "Walked around all those make-up counters and sniffed the 'try me' bottles. Some of those saleswomen watched me like I was a thief. Yeesh, even a thief wouldn't want some of that stinky stuff. But this one made me think of you, Mom, and the lady there was really nice. She asked a lot of questions."

"What questions?" I was trying to picture him at a perfume counter. He was 'all boy.' His little fingers always sticky with mud or cookies. As he grew, the smudges changed to grease and crankcase oil, and those curious fingers could undo anything he put his hands to. Following his dad around, watching intently, he learned to put them back together.

"She asked why I liked this perfume. I told her it was sweet, but fierce also, like my mom. She runs a tight ship. It's not smushy sweet like the junk ole nasty lips over there has. I think she's guarding her bottles, not trying to sell 'um."

"I see," the lady said.

I'm sure 'the lady' was trying not to smile as hard as I was.

"How much is this?" I asked her. She put several bottles on the counter. The biggest was twenty, one was twelve, and a little one was seven. I wanted to get the big bottle for you, Mom, but then I wouldn't have enough for Dad's gift."

This one is so honest. He would never make it as a thief.

"The lady said if it was a perfume you loved and wore often, the bigger bottle would be nice. But it's best to try a little one first."

"Yes," I said, "This one is new to me. You made a great choice."

"Mom, do you know a perfume can smell different on skin? It may not be as nice as it smells in the bottle."

How I wanted to smother this little man with hugs and kisses. But the time for that was passing, 'smoochy stuff' no longer welcome.

He watched, bouncing on his toes as I opened the little bottle. "Let's see." I sprayed some on my wrist. I sniffed the scent on my wrist then held out my arm. "What do you think?"

He made a great inhale and grinned, although I suspected he wanted to jump up and down. "I knew it. You smell wonderful." He ran off to check if his dad liked his gift. I knew my husband would love whatever it was, so I had no worry my little guy's heart would be damaged.

I gave a stern "Be nice" glance to Sylvia, his younger sister, who watched us from her place beside the Christmas tree. Her teasing could be on the bitter side, although I knew she adored the finger puppets he had given her.

"I'm just telling the truth!" she would proclaim. "You tell me to always be honest," she would slam down her hand. "If something is ugly, it's ugly."

When I answered that someone else might find it pretty, she ignored my advice. I feared she was headed for a difficult life.

"Let her be." My other half said. "One day, she'll find someone she wants to be nice to and learn compassion." She did, but that's another story.

I wore this scent when I wanted to be the Nice Lady. It's a scent for the steady wife who held down the fort while her husband went about the business of protecting the skies of this world. Not one for the long days a no-nonsense teacher installed this world's history into teenage minds, nor quite an aroma for seducing said husband.

Definitely not one for the word smith who told stories that claimed a place on bookshelves.

It was not used very often, but especially when I thought of my earnest young boy and his joyful Christmas of giving gifts with his own money. And definitely when that young man comes to visit with his own son.

I held the little bottle, almost empty now. No, not empty, for it held the memory of a young boy and how he grew into a kind and gentle son, now husband and father.

Will everything I touch spring memories at me? How could I let it all go? I need another cup of coffee.

I yearn to stay where the memories warm my heart. But this house has been sold, and the new one is purchased and waiting for me to arrive. Unless I want my friends and my two, local, lovable but opinionated children to make these decisions for me, I best get busy. But coffee first.

On my way to the kitchen, I glanced at the antique bureau under the huge mirror in the entranceway. More memories flooded in. The scent of beeswax and lemon polish mixed with the aroma of bay candles said Christmas Eve.

My mother found that bureau under a pile of trash in a corner of my grandmother's cellar, under broken chairs, mildewed boots, bottles, and other oddments. I remember that basement with a shudder. Talk about a place the Addams family would have loved. The stairs were rickety with no railing. One light bulb swung by a cord draped over a large nail hammered onto an overhead beam.

The 'floor' was bricks embedded in the dirt, ever gritty and a bit damp. It's where Gram kept potatoes and other things that needed to 'winter over.' I wasn't often allowed down there for fear I would 'take a tumble,' so of course, I had to prove I was of stronger stuff. Don't think I fooled anyone when I came tearing up the steps as if the hounds of hell were after me. I can still recall the musty smell.

When Mom cleared the cellar after Gram went to live in the senior center, she quipped that as she emptied that corner, she hoped there wasn't a body buried at the bottom of it.

There wasn't; there was this bureau. Now, my mother never met an antique she couldn't love back to better days. She hauled it home, applied all her skill in refurbishing it, and set it proudly between our kitchen and dining area. Dad frequently muttered 'it's in the way,' but knew better than suggest Mom part with it.

Now I inherited it. With its deeply carved cabinet drawers, it greets folks in the entranceway, topped by my MIL's gilt and marble clock and candlesticks. The $90 bronze framed mirror on the wall above tries to look like it belongs, but hey, that was a bit pricey in the '70s. It's an antique now, I'm told.

I remember the first time Anna, my son Michael's fiancé, visited. Even with all the Christmas trimmings and glitter about the house, she was drawn to that bureau like a magnet. Over the years, she learned the history and was always the first to open the crotchety old drawers to get the silver chest for holiday dinners.

From their overseas military assignments, she has collected a lot of beautiful furniture, so I've no idea where she will put it. But when she inherits it, those firewood panel doors are in for the polishing of their lives.

Ah, firewood. The piano. I'm a mediocre player but do enjoy it for the sense of peace. I'll have room for it in my new home, so it's a keeper. Eventually, it's for a grandson, but he's still in college with no room for an old upright piano yet. But ... I can see that long ago little boy, barely big enough to climb onto the bench. Most little folks pound on the keys, enjoying the ability to make noise. But this one plunked the keys gently, laughing for the joy of it. When he was about five, I recognized he played a repeating melody. I showed him a score sheet and asked him to play it slowly, so I could write the notes down so he could save the melody.

"Like a page in a book anyone can read?" he asked and promptly named it 'Down Water Happiness.' Over the years, whenever he came to my home, he aimed straight for the piano, playing softly. He now plays a synthesizer, guitar, and even played French horn in junior high band. He knows the piano will be his one day. It's enough for now.

THE DOORBELL PULLED me out of my memories. Brad and Sylvia, our two children who live nearby, announced they came to 'help.'

"I think we need to have a garage sale, Mom," Sylvia said.

"Count me out. And Mom, too. She doesn't need the stress. I mean it, Sis." Brad, my ever-practical son, hammered his hands in the air to make his point.

"Look, I make a living organizing stuff. First, we'll only offer things for sale that Mom doesn't want, doesn't like, and doesn't ever want to see again."

I listened to them bicker for a few minutes, thinking of some monstrosities I only keep because they were gifts. I often wonder if the giver was as glad to get rid of it as I—"

"What's second, Sis?"

"I get first pick." Sylvia brandished her tablet at him like a sword. "Who knows, maybe one of Mom's horrors is my delight, or yours, big bad brother." The last was said with lots of teeth.

"—and you're no Riding Hood." Brad's response to their old game. "No way we're picking over Mom's stuff like a team of ghouls."

"Children, children, stop. A sale for stuff I don't want sounds fine, although I don't want strangers walking through my house. But ... how can I sell something someone gave me if they might come to the sale?"

"Like that 'Leg' lamp cousin Jolly gave Dad?" Brad shook his head, his eyes dancing. "He comes every Christmas and preens over that lamp. I thought Dad was going to fall over laughing when he opened the box. And when he plugged it in, and the skirt did the hula? It's a prime garage sale pick."

"But what if Jolly finds out I sold it?"

"Humm, you could send it back with a note 'cause you know how much he loved it,'" Brad said.

"Yeah, he doesn't have one because his wife won't allow it. But if I return it—" We all dissolved in giggles, picturing Aunt Verona's reaction.

"Okay. Brad, you pack and mail it to dear cousin Jolly. All Mom has to do is write the kind note." Sylvia was in her organizing element.

"Speaking of the garage, you need to keep a lot of the gardening tools," Brad said, "because we'll create a new garden. Even if you hire a mowing company, you'll need rakes, clippers, trowels, and other stuff. I know you will be digging in the dirt there. My housewarming gift to you is a small storage shed. It will fit in the back corner of the yard, with a potting shelf. And your roses, too," he added with a big grin.

I took a deep breath and blinked to keep the tears at bay. "They won't transplant, dear. I know that. It would kill them. The new owner said she loved roses and would enjoy caring for mine because she had to leave hers at their previous home."

"Mom, hold on to this. I have a friend of a friend who owns a nursery. They 'bud' roses all the time. When I explained your roses came from the Jersey 'Rose Man,' she offered to reproduce yours if she could keep some for her business. She only needs to take cuttings from your roses to bud her two-year ready stock. Mom, don't cry."

"Brad ... that's ... beyond wonderful. I'll still have my roses, young and vibrant like my new home. I know where I want to put an arbor so that the tops of the climbers will fall over the fence, visible from the street." I stood and grabbed him for a hug, finding joy in the move for the first time. In a few years, my roses would again gift their aroma to my small yard as family and friends gathered under the arbor.

"You know, I think I still have one of those imported German knives my dad used to bud roses. I think it's in a box in the top drawer of dad's bureau. It might make a nice thank you since she knows about our 'rose man.'"

"Wow, she's a practical no-nonsense businesswoman, but she gushed over my connection to Grandad's roses. The knife is perfect thank you. She refused any payment, said it would be an honor. She can't wait to get the cuttings."

"I'll invite her for an afternoon, bore her with your grand-dad's slides and notebooks. I'm keeping most of them for you and the grandkids, but I could give her a few pictures. Maybe to use in an advertisement, or she could borrow some. I suspect she will want to see where I want to plant them and supervise that. But—"

"Mom, that's all great. Let's get back to the sale," Sylvia hugged me. "When do you want to do a walkabout to tag the large furnishings you don't want?"

"Time's getting short. So best do it soon—like tomorrow if you have time?" She consulted her 'life on a wrist' as I called it. "My last client is 2:00 p.m., so I'll be here about three. That work for you?"

"Yes, and I'll take a short walk in the morning with a paper tablet to make a list. There is one big problem—"

"Mom, please don't fret. Well, no more than you usually do. Brad and I are here. And Aunt Jane is anxious to help but doesn't want to intrude or get in the way. She'd be great at the cash register, dealing with people who want to haggle over prices. Some folks will feel cheated if they don't get to bargain. That's become a thing with garage sales.

"Now, what's got you fretting, little momma?" Brad braced one hand on my head to hold me off. It was a reference to the first time in his teens that his arms were longer than mine.

"All the glassware, china pieces, stuff I've inherited? Both of your grandmas were avid collectors and left boxes and boxes of stuff for me. I have no idea whether a piece is valuable or just something they liked. Like that green depression-ware thing shaped like a floppy hat? I think it's supposed to be a plant holder, but gracious, it's ugly. But is it valuable? I've no idea. How can I ever price it if I don't know what it's worth?"

"Oh, I thought it's a major problem. No offense, but it's simple," Sylvia said. "Price it a bit more than you would pay for it, if you happened to want it for some odd reason. If you would never pay more than five dollars, that's the price. So what if some glass expert happens by, spies a prize, sees the bargain price, then beats it to the register, eager to purchase it for only five dollars? When she walks off grinning with her 'precious,' well, you've made someone's day."

"I'll probably make several days. I'll watch for those grins. But ... who's going to price, move stuff outside, or arrange it?" I hated hearing my whiney voice. "I can't lift—"

"Hold off, Mom. Uncle Travis will help Sam and I with the toting, and you do have several grandchildren who need family time with you. They will most certainly help," Brad intoned with his deep 'father' voice. "But an offer of dinner—?"

"No problem. Let's do a last Italian Cook-Off in this old house. A send-off with the aroma of tomatoes, garlic, and spices. That will give me a chance to see what kitchen items need to go into the new house for all our next get-togethers. One of the big selling points for that house is all the space in my new kitchen. Now ... enough of this. I know you two have busy days."

"Mom, we love you and want you to be happy," Sylvia said.

"Strangely, these plans have made me happy. I'm going to like my new home, with the stuff I truly love around me."

I caught the relieved looks that passed between my two kids and realized they were also worried about this.

The next afternoon, Sylvia breezed in. "I'm here for the 'Ugly Day Walkabout.'" She brought out her ever-present electronic list maker, stickies, and her 'just for fun' ink pens.

"Why the different color stickies?"

"Yellow is for Out, 'Out to the yellow brick road garage sale.' Blue is for 'I'll bust fingers if you touch it.' Pink's for 'embarrassed 'cause I can't decide.'"

"Let's begin, back rooms to front, then upstairs, leaving the basement for last. Brad will do the garage and tool shed." She hugged me. "You still okay for this?"

"I think so. Not sure I'm up for all the hours this will take."

"Relax. We'll take breaks. Sammy and Jane—you do recall your grandkids?" At my scowl, she continued, "They're bringing pizza around five and will help in the garage. Relax, we've got this. No stress, you hear? If it gets too much, we're sending you to your brother's in California to lounge on the beach and watch the hot Navy SEALS run past. You'll return tan and ready to see your new home with everything in place. Or not in the right place, so you can boss us around until we fix it. Got that?"

We began in the master bedroom. "Okay, first, I plan to take my bedroom furniture and most of the clothes in my closet—"

"Except?" Sylvia asked, her eyes trying not to stray to her dad's clothes.

"I know. I know. Maybe that's why I'm dragging my feet. But it's time to do something about Dad's clothes and stuff. I ... I just don't want to ..." I gathered my strength. Time to let go of some of his belongings.

"Mom, how about this? Put everything you want to keep in the bins I brought. Then give Brad time in here alone to take whatever he wants, the grandkids, also. If you aren't sure about anything, just keep it. You do have an attic in that new house, you know."

"Want to keep the stinky golf or bowling shoes?" she peered into the closet.

"No, but I'll keep my bowling ball since it's sized for me and wouldn't fit anyone else. Maybe I'll find a singles league ... I did enjoy bowling." I felt more than heard Sylvia's sigh of relief and hated all the worry I had put on my children with my insistence on putting my head in the sand, ignoring what needed to be done after my husband passed. At least, I hope I was making progress.

An hour later, Brad came in smelling of grass clippings and gasoline to announce they had cleared a corner of the garage to store items I'd need at my new home.

"I came in to ask what you want to do with the Harley."

I thought I'd held up pretty well on the walkabout, reasonable and not too emotional, but his question took the wind out of me. I collapsed onto the sofa, hands on my head as if to hold in the memories piling on, all the places, the friends, the fun. My husband and I had so many good times on that bike. I didn't want to part with it, but how could I keep it? It took up a lot of space, and the truth is I would never be able to ride it again. But what to do with it? I looked up to find Brad grinning.

"You're going to make me ask for it, aren't you?"

"You really want that old thing?"

"I've wanted it since I was old enough to sneak into the garage to climb onto it and dream of all the places I'd go, like in the Dr. Seuss book you used to read to us." He shook his head as if to brace himself, as he did as a child when he feared his father was about to deny a longed-for hope.

"I ... I'm ... Brad, of course, you can have the Beast. On one condition."

"Anything."

"Dad and I kept a journal of the places, people, fun, and the painful times, too. Now you have to add your travels."

"Lisa and I will be thrilled to keep up that tradition."

I went to the hall chest and rummaged in the top drawer for the keys and tossed them to Brad.

107

"I need to take it for a spin around the block to check it out." He left with a jaunty step, new owner of a Harley that still had miles of life to share with him.

"Hey, Sam, grab a helmet. We have to check out our bike."

"Oh, man, yee-haw!" was the answer as I heard the familiar growl.

"Well, he always steals the limelight," Sylvia said.

"And, we've had a lovely afternoon. Time for a break. How about a glass of wine with crackers on the deck?"

"Do I hear wine and snacks are available here?" Sylvia's husband, ever the stealthy one, slipped into the room to give his wife a kiss and me a hug.

"Hi, Grant, only if you uncork a bottle and carry stuff out. I'll be waiting on the porch." I returned his hug and swanned outside to let them organize the treats. Knowing Grant, it would include salted nuts and bread for dipping into something tasty.

I sat to enjoy the evening. My new home had a patio, but now it would have roses, the scents of beeswax and tomato sauce, and the sunsets would still be glorious.

TRACE AMOUNTS

TERRA LUFT

Adult Fiction

*H*ow had I gotten so lucky? This breakfast nook, in this restored old house, in a neighborhood I'd been dreaming of living in forever. It still didn't seem real, even as I sat here in the new place. Our new place. I watched the birds flitting from branch to branch in the tree outside the window and tried to ignore all the boxes still left to unpack in the kitchen. Sipping my first cup of coffee, I silently thanked the me of yesterday for this moment of morning solitude. I had insisted last night on having this one corner of the kitchen cleared of chaos and set up before we quit to sleep on the mattress on the floor. The fluorite and citrine stones on the windowsill had brought peace and lightness to the space while we slept.

"Good morning, my love," Darren kissed the top of my head on his way past. "The coffee smells divine."

"Mmmm … morning," I said, smiling over at him past the stack of boxes while he bustled with the most important area of the kitchen, the coffee station. "The last box packed, and the first one unpacked. Worth it!"

"Hm. Also worth this morning's backache to have this spot to enjoy it in. Great call." He sat down next to me and pulled his phone out of his pocket for his morning ritual with the daily news.

"I was just thinking that," I said, looking back out the window. I pushed the list of things we had to do today to the back of my mind and basked in experiencing the first morning in our new home, the coffee mug warming my hands. A gentle breeze blew in through the open window bringing with it the smells of the morning: the new leaves on trees, growing grass, dew-moistened soil, and everything alive outside the window. I could definitely get used to this every morning. The energy of the house wrapped around me with promises of happiness and contentment.

"Some of the guys will be here in about half an hour. I'll need your input on where you want a lot of the furniture. You're the one with the vision about this place," Darren said, bringing me back from my waking meditation.

"I know it's older than you wanted, but hopefully, you'll barely notice that when everything is moved in, and all these boxes are unpacked," I replied. When I saw this place, I knew I was meant to live here.

"There aren't a lot of modern options in this part of the city, and I do love the convenience of being close to the office."

"I can't wait to be settled and start exploring the neighborhood. Tiana will be here later to help unpack the kitchen boxes once the furniture is all in place. Guess I better get dressed." I leaned in for a kiss, the taste of shared coffee on our lips.

I walked through the house, looking past the modern updates. Mostly empty like this, it was easy to see the size and shape of its original skeleton as built in the late 1950s. The small rooms had been updated, accent walls of shiplap giving it a modern look, and additions giving it extra space, but remnants of how it must have looked originally still existed.

Standing in the bathroom, I swore I could see the original pink countertops hinted at by the built-in wood-on-wood drawers behind the door. Sure, someone could have ripped those out instead of painting over them and made room for a double vanity, but then where would we store all the linens?

I finished brushing my teeth and smiled at my reflection in the mirror. The possibilities of this place and the happiness of the future pressed in on me with anticipatory weight.

The bedroom felt like another gauntlet of boxes as I made my way to the suitcase I had packed to live out of the first few days, a life hack I discovered online years ago when I was in my starving artist move-every-six-months phase. I crouched to pick out clothes and stopped as a faint whiff of old-fashioned perfume hit me solidly in the nose. I hadn't smelled anything like it in years.

I closed my eyes to focus only on the scent while warm memories flooded my mind. Summers in the garden as a child and afternoons at the table eating tuna sandwiches with butter. It wasn't exactly the same, but the heavy notes of rose and jasmine reminded me of my grandmother. This scent had an underlying hint of something else, too. Cigarette smoke?

I opened my eyes and gasped at the lavender shag carpet under my feet where the cream bedroom carpet should have been. The long skinny threads moved as I ran my fingers across it. I glanced up and saw glittery popcorn ceilings of the past where the smooth texture should be. How was this possible? I looked back down at the pastel shag.

"Jess, you okay?"

I squealed and jumped almost out of my skin. "You scared the shit out of me!" The antique carpet vanished, along with the scent.

"I didn't mean to," Darren said from the doorway while my heart tried to pound out of my chest.

"Don't sneak up on me." He raised his hands in a calming gesture that made me feel like a cornered animal, which seemed ridiculous even to me. The vision had shaken me, which didn't usually happen.

"Sneak up on you? Babe, I've been calling your name for ten minutes. The guys are here. *Are* you okay?" Darren asked from the doorway.

"What? No, I just left you in the kitchen and came straight up here to get dressed." The memory of purple shag carpeting flashed in my mind's eye and stopped me from further protesting.

"That was thirty minutes ago, and you're still not dressed." He gestured at me standing there in my bathrobe to back up his point.

"The weirdest thing just happened ..." I mentally retraced my steps looking for an explanation for the time loss. I'd had visions before, but never lost time. Could this be a new layer of my fledgling clairvoyant talents?

"Tell me about it later? I need you decent and downstairs, so we know where to put all the biggest furniture." He turned to go, and I caught an almost-there whiff of 1950s perfume again.

THE WARMTH of the sun and the morning light of the enclosed porch had become my favorite place to paint after Darren left for the office since we'd settled in. Darren also loved it, but we'd come to an arrangement on the designated use for the beautiful space that made us both happy. I had claimed the far half of the room as a permanent location for my easel and most of my paints. The patio furniture and occasional cigar smoking activities Darren preferred were more suitable for the evening, when the light had long passed the golden hour. A perfect balance between both of us.

The energy of the house had settled in around me the last few weeks and inspired what I thought silently in my heart could be the beginnings of something special. That is, if I let myself think such thoughts—which I would never dream of doing for fear of jinxing it all. Right now, it was the beginning of a series of paintings inspired by the pastel color pallets of the 1950s I'd caught a glimpse of during our move. I envisioned others all tied together loosely, all created on this porch, representing the color pallets of the different eras the house had endured. Others could decide what to make of them; I just painted what I felt. The house and the strong energy from its long history had done wonders for my art.

I reached for the dregs of my morning coffee that had gone cold next to me while I'd been lost in thought and my creating. There were worse things than losing track of time while painting something I could feel proud of. Cold coffee had become the norm out here, and I couldn't really complain about it since it was a small price to pay. I debated the question of what tea to drink this afternoon as I walked through the sitting room that had once been a carport, judging by the rest of the houses on the street. I glanced out the giant picture window overlooking the covered back patio to the terraced gardens beyond. So much beauty here.

In the kitchen, I looked out over the same view through the smaller window over the sink, still feeling lucky we had found this place. That's when it hit me, the unmistakable scent of old perfume and cigarettes. I'd caught faint hints of it a couple of times since that first morning here. Those times it had been like walking into a room where someone had been wearing it hours ago. This time it hit me like a visceral thing, as if I'd just sprayed the fragrance with a heavy hand. I turned, expecting to see someone standing in the kitchen with me, but I was alone.

Goosebumps prickled my arms, and the hair stood up on the back of my neck. My heart rate and breathing increased, remembering the still unexplained loss of time when I had last fully smelled this scent. I turned slowly around the kitchen, still expecting to see someone else here.

I saw no one, but I swore I felt a presence with me. I breathed deeply, trying to stay calm, which only increased the strength of the scent in my nose. After my first vision, I researched clairalience, part of the range of psychic talents connected to scent, which, until that time, I had never encountered. I had experienced enough psychic activity that it wasn't beyond my imagination, though.

"Hello, is anyone there?" I said to the empty room. No one answered, but I still felt like someone was there with me. "Please make yourself known. It's okay."

I reached out with my psychic self to connect with the energy and realized it felt familiar. It embodied the energy of the house around me that I'd been channeling into my art. I smiled and leaned into the experience.

The edge of my vision reflected a change in the inset glass window of the stainless steel refrigerator door. I didn't see another person, but the reflection did not match the room behind me. It looked like a glimpse into the past. I tried not to move my eyes, just in case it disappeared while looking closer. My heart pounded with excitement and wonder. Instead of the modern archway into the new addition, a wall of dark wood paneling with a small door reduced the room to a tiny area that held a low table and two antique chairs tucked into the corner. Instead of the sleek kitchen cabinets and double oven lining the side wall, there were antiquated wooden ones that looked like they were from the 1970s and a squat, dark-colored refrigerator. Looking at the mismatched rooms gave me vertigo, but I was also afraid to blink in case the vision vanished.

I shifted a little to my right to see more of the older kitchen in the reflection. Instead of the open area where my modern kitchen met the dining room and flowed into the open living area, I saw an old paneled hallway leading toward the original living room at the front of the house. The scent of perfume had faded, but it matched the era of this older version of the house I saw. I could see *and* smell the past here.

I turned away from the reflection and walked slowly toward the front of the house, hoping that I could find the old room in another reflection and also hoping to catch a glimpse of whatever guided my artistic energy from this fixed location tied to the past. Maybe it wasn't a person, but the house itself. I held on to the lingering scent that was quickly fading from the air. The smell spurred me on down the ghostly hallway as if inviting me to follow.

The excitement of what else I might see as I traveled down this clairvoyant path thrilled me. I had no idea why I was seeing these things, but the imagery was definitely tied to the creative work I'd been doing since we'd settled in. I felt the familiarity of it swirling around me, evoking the same nostalgia I'd channeled into my painting. The need to see more and understand it compelled me. Like I did with most things, I plunged headlong and hoped for the best.

I rounded the corner into the living room, still catching the faintest whisper of perfume hanging in the air. Walking slowly past the picture window overlooking the street, I kept my eyes ahead, searching down the hallway for more signs of that hidden world of the past. Here, the honey oak and mauves of 1980s decor greeted me where I knew my modern furnishings stood. Like discovering peeling layers of linoleum and wallpaper during a remodel.

"Hey, babe, where you going?" Darren's voice from behind

me stopped me in my tracks and brought me crashing solidly back to the here and now from where I'd been. My psychic self and my physical self, somehow suspended between now and the glimpse of all that the house had been, pulled at the edges of my consciousness as if each fought to win a tug-o-war.

"Oooooh," The word escaped me like a sigh filled with wonder. "I just had the most amazing experience. A tangible glimpse into the past and the energy I've been channeling into my latest art project." My hands shook while I tried to convey all I had just experienced. I didn't know where to start.

"Is this another new-age adventure?" He smiled at me with indulgence, but at least he didn't discount it. I loved him all the more for it.

"Yes! I know for sure now that it's the energy of the house that's behind my current paintings. It felt the same—"

"Babe, hold that thought while I drop my stuff in my office. Then we'll open a bottle of wine, and you can tell me everything."

I smiled, nodding my acceptance. As he turned, I caught the faintest odor of rotting peaches. How could there be rotten fruit in the house? As quickly as I thought it, the scent was gone.

THE MORNING, full of promise and perfect lighting, had only frustrated me. Why was this particular painting, the final in the series and full of all that I could feel it wanted to be, fighting me?

I closed my eyes and grounded myself with a deep breath inward, reaching for the creative energy I'd tapped into while the first four paintings had sprung to life here on the sun porch. Those pieces had become a visual and abstract embodiment of the house, our dream home. From the pastel pinks and lavenders of the 1950s in the first painting to the burnt orange and avocado greens of the '70s in the second, the forest green and mauves of the '90s dominated the third piece, then the clean lines of the black and white—with a splash of red for accent—that embodied the current version of the house represented in the fourth. The series walked a viewer through the colorful transformation of a dwelling through time.

All I had left was this, the largest piece, meant to represent the house itself which had cradled decades and myriad lives within its walls. I would display it in the center with the other four arranged around it. But it kept turning dark. Full of anguish. Of ending. Morning after morning, I sat here in front of the easel, rejecting what I felt and willing different inspiration. Fighting what I felt in my heart the work demanded. My art, as usual, refused to be negotiated with. But I was a stubborn bitch, too.

I stepped away from the easel and turned my back on the blankness of what I had scraped off and painted over yesterday. My mind's eye, my artist's eye, could still see the dark swirls under the gesso, still feel in my heart what the last attempt had left me with as if lurking just below the surface. It permeated. I couldn't escape it.

I fought the urge to scream and sweep all my paints and brushes from the table. That would only waste supplies and make me more furious. I had to get to the root of what was blocking me, or I would never get past it to finish the series. The series which I had scheduled to display in three months at my gallery show.

I went into troubleshooting mode instead. Maybe I needed to cleanse my creative energy, so the house energy could shine through again. A change of pace. A new project. New setting. New intentions. Maybe this particular series was only four paintings instead of the five I had planned for in the beginning. I could tie it to the four seasons and call it finished. Forget whatever this last painting meant to conjure from my psyche. No one but me would know I had intended the series to be five paintings.

As much as I wanted that to be possible, longed for it as an easy way through this current creative crossroads, I knew this war within myself was because the last canvas had to be part of the series. I felt it calling me, demanding. Knew it needed to be finished just as much as the others. The energy of creation felt unfinished. Yet I also feared to go where that energy was taking me.

The first four paintings in this series had emerged fast and furious and full of life. The last dragged and dipped toward darkness. Something had changed. I assumed the house itself had been driving the first four paintings because they had just happened after settling from the move, tied to the psychic flashes that connected me with the past. I'd been so sure it was the house itself in the energy I'd been channeling, but now that was gone, just like the visions. If the creative spark had come from the house, then what the hell was this new energy all about?

"Still struggling with that last one, huh?" Darren handed me a cup of tea as I entered the kitchen.

The scent of rotten peaches, something no one but me ever smelled and which I'd come to dread the last few weeks, hit me full force. I lowered my nose to the teacup and inhaled deeply to mask it. "Mmmm. Peppermint. How did you know?" I opened my eyes to meet his and convey my gratitude over the top of the rim.

He shrugged. "I pay attention. Your afternoon choice of tea matches how your day has gone. Peppermint when you're frustrated, cinnamon when you're happy, chamomile when you're sad." He leaned against the granite countertop, still dressed for the office and looking tired.

I'd gotten lucky when I found him. He showed his love every

day in little and surprising ways, like paying attention to what tea I needed at the end of the day. Our life here in this house notched my contentment to levels I never knew were possible. The future ahead of us warmed me like the afternoon sun on our beloved porch.

"Are you not going to play basketball today?" It was Wednesday, and he never missed time on the court.

"Nah, I'm feeling really rundown today. I just wanted to come home and spend a quiet night on the couch together, if that's good with you." He stepped toward me and wrapped his arms around my waist.

The cloying scent of rotten fruit was all I could think about as I opened my arms wide to return the hug.

I CLUNG to the unrelenting numbness as I stood before the completed canvas that had haunted me from the first time I had tried to paint it all those many weeks ago. I stared at what many whispers in the art world had already labeled my 'crowning artistic achievement,' and shoved down all the emotions it threatened to overwhelm me with. The swirls of midnight blue contrasting with the harsh angles, melting into the hinted-at outlines of threatening figures. All of it sat at the back of my throat like a scream on the edge of release.

This last canvas, that once had haunted and frustrated me, had now become a known harbinger of all that had come. Only in hindsight did I understand what had changed. My clairvoyant visions of the house were really only behind the first three paintings. The fourth painting clearly represented the present. My clairalient scents tied to this ... this ... *monstrosity* ... represented my future. The house had been trying to warn me, but I hadn't understood until it was too late.

How could I have known?

I couldn't look away.

I couldn't move.

I refused to feel.

Finally, I turned my back to it.

People came up to me, remarking on how wonderful my art was and how much they loved it. As if they couldn't see it for the visual representation of my world collapsing that it so clearly was. My agent on one side, Tiana, my dearest friend on the other, both tried their best to fill my silence with murmured thank yous to those who filed by as I stared blankly past everyone.

Let them think what they liked; I was beyond caring about anything now.

I had nothing but the gaping hole in my world where Darren had been until a month ago. Six weeks since I'd learned it was too late to save him from the cancer that would steal him from me and our future together. It felt like a lifetime.

And now, all I had was this fucking painting with its tiny, unassuming plaque declaring the title *I didn't want to worry you*. They were the words Darren had said when our life had changed forever.

I longed to smell the dying scent of rotten peaches just one last time.

I REMEMBER

R. E. BEEBE

Memoir

*P*sychologists say that, of the five senses, smell evokes memories more than any other. Scents are tied to emotions that help a person recall events decades later. Many such memories last a lifetime, even when dementia has stolen a person's identity or when the ability to smell is lost. Knowing that makes me grateful because scent is about much more than the actual smell.

One night, when I simply could not sleep, memories began flowing through my mind ...

I REMEMBER COFFEE AND CIGARETTES, which were unusual and intriguing during my childhood because it was only Grandma Red who was allowed to smoke in our house. Her visits were rare since she lived in faraway Kansas. When I was young, she was the only one I knew who would regularly take my dad down a notch with her quick, biting wit. Ever-ready with her, "you dummy," whenever he did something she disagreed with, coupled with her bright laughter, made us kids stare wide-eyed and wonder why he never contradicted her. The scent of laughter.

I remember cinnamon and warm butter as my sister and I watched with fascination while Mom transformed flour and milk into heaven. We waited eagerly for the dough to rise. Once I simply couldn't wait and climbed on a kitchen chair to steal a piece of cinnamon roll. Mom put cookie sheets on top of the fridge, so the dough would rise faster. My sister snitched on me but, instead of getting mad, Mom smiled, then reached for the pan and gave us both a fat piece of dough slick with butter and cinnamon. The scent of love.

I remember the smell of silicone and wood glue from the garage when Dad was building bookshelves and how wonderful it was for him to let me hang around and help even though I mostly got in the way. The scent of patience.

I remember holding our family dog Sam close, breathing in the smell of him while I cried my heart out because we had both lost my cat D.C.—short for Damn Cat—who was our other best friend. The scent of comfort.

I remember the sharp metal smell of roller skates at the rink on Saturdays when it was packed wall-to-wall with people. Plus, the distinct smell of popcorn that Dad rarely bought for us but pervaded the theater anyway while he dozed through the movie. It was special because he was so busy and gave up his Saturdays to be with us. The scent of time well spent.

I remember the clean, wet, soapy smell of the big white sheets when Grandma Hollingsworth would let me help her send them through the roller, and the smell of sugar and icing when we made cookies every Christmas. The scent of happiness.

I remember hot summer days and sultry evenings walking past fields of freshly cut hay or pedaling our bikes down the street on a Saturday morning past fathers mowing their lawns until the entire street was filled with the fresh, clean aroma of newly cut grass. The scent of innocence.

I remember cold sweat, bad breath, and lust when a family friend became a monster and hurt me badly. The scent of terror.

I remember the stink of our little dog Bo's foot. He had a cut in it that seemed insignificant but became septic and took his life shortly after. The scent of death.

I remember hot tar and sweat when my best friend and I walked home barefoot in July because the mare we were riding had enough of us, dumped us off on the school lawn, and galloped merrily home. The scent of comradery.

I remember the smell of black licorice when I met my mom's new boyfriend. He carried them in his pocket because he was trying to stop smoking. He soon became our stepdad and brought with him an unexpected world of acceptance as well as decades of happiness. The scent of joy.

I remember ammonia, leather, shavings, and hay overlayed with the smell of horses that permeates the air in the barn and brings my heart joy. The scent of soul-deep peace.

I remember the smell of musk and male from early adventures making out with boyfriends, which later became the feeling of comfort and safety lying next to my husband in bed or embraced in his arms. Even though I couldn't sense the actual smell, my brain knew. The scent of two hearts beating as one.

If my eyes are closed, I can go back to the simple pleasures of sitting on the porch steps on sultry summer days eating a peanut butter sandwich, and I swear I can still taste the strawberry jam.

Ah, such memories. It's amazing how long they linger. Scents I can still remember decades after losing my sense of smell.

That's right, I can't smell a thing. Not even a skunk. It can be both annoying and often humorous at the same time. How did this happen, you might ask. Well …

When I was in my late teens, I had a job as an exercise rider for racehorses. That morning, the trainer wanted to gate school his filly, so we put her in the gates. She was very nervous and kept moving. She was scared, and the gates were just too enclosed, and they make strange noises. The filly couldn't go forward with the gate closed, for good reason. The front is too tall for most horses to jump over from a standstill. She felt she had to go somewhere, so she jumped backward. When they do that in the gates, they usually squish the jockey underneath.

She flipped me off her back when she reared up, and my helmet hit the gate with a loud bang. Luckily, our friend Clyde was the header. He reached over and jerked me out of there before the horse could smash me any more than she already had.

At first, I thought all I'd come away with were a few bruises. I slept most of that day away and then thought I was okay. It was a couple of weeks before I realized there was more wrong than that. When I tipped my head back, I would get dizzy. Finally, I went to get X-rays. It turned out my neck bones were straight—they're supposed to have a curve in them, and the nerves in my neck were being pinched due to severe whiplash. If something had hit the top of my head with even a little force, it would have severed my spine.

That was the end of my job galloping racehorses. It took a few months for a chiropractor to get my neck bones in the right shape again. It also took me a while to realize that I had lost my sense of smell.

It's sort of an invisible problem and can be rather inconvenient. Like when the wall heater in the tiny house we lived in had a gas leak. I had been getting headaches for a couple of weeks and couldn't pinpoint why. My chair was right in front of the heater. Robert was a smoker, so his sense of smell was not too great either. My sister came to visit, took one step in the door, and said, "You have a gas leak."

I think my family often fibs to me when they say dinner tastes good. After all, I can't tell one flavor from another. The only things I can taste are sweet, sour, bitter, and salt. I do remember what things tasted like, but if my eyes were closed, I doubt I could tell you what I was eating if the texture didn't give it away.

The lack of a sense of smell lends itself to some humorous moments. My husband claims it's the reason we stayed married since I couldn't tell if he smelled bad. It's probably why I get along so well with critters, too.

I can't tell if dogs smell bad, either. Our old English Mastiff, Gene (named after Gene Upshaw, lineman for the Oakland Raiders), was known to clear a room when she cut loose with a fart, and I'm oblivious.

But my greatest fear when it comes to no sense of smell came true a few years ago. I had always worried about the dogs getting skunked and me letting them in the house. Skunks are a frequent hazard when you live in the country and own dumb dogs.

One night at four in the morning, Gene insisted on going out, so I let her out the door and waited for her to bark to come back in. Luckily, when I let her in, she went straight over to Robert's side of the bed. He woke out of a sound sleep and exclaimed, "What reeks?"

Yep, she'd been skunked. I promptly put her back outside. Then I found we didn't have the ingredients in the house to wash her with, so I drove to Walmart and got them. If you don't know the recipe, it's one part baking soda, one part hydrogen peroxide, and a little bit of dish soap. You need a *lot* of hydrogen peroxide and baking soda for a dog the size of Gene. It works well if the smell hasn't settled in. At least that's what they tell me when I'm done washing the dogs and our clothes. Maybe they're lying?

As I lay in bed contemplating those memories, tears rolled down my cheeks. Tears full of gratitude, joy, and good, clean fun. I realized that, even though I lost my sense of smell forty years ago, if I quiet my mind and concentrate, I remember.

THE RESISTANCE, A LOVE STORY

J. ALAN GIFT

Experimental Fiction

*a*n immense blimp cast a shadow over cowering skyscrapers as radical socialists took the city. Confused pigeons slammed into windows. Air Raid sirens screamed in reverse. Grown men soiled themselves. Fleeing, wide-eyed conspiracy theorists crowded the sidewalk, running in one direction, pushing me, jostling me, spinning me like a drunken ballerina.

"Move, you idiot!"

"Get out of the way, you Puke Face!"

"Potato Head!"

"Worm Breath!"

"Zit Pus!"

Frantic teenagers searching for meaning spun me into a dark alley and SPLAT! I was sprayed and splashed with iced ammonia, burning my face like sizzling bacon spit while angry hornets flew up my nose. A net fell over me. I was dragged into a dimly lit room.

"That's not him!" someone yelled. "You glue sniffing morons!

Not even the right species! Where's his feathers? Where are his two-toed feet? He's not foaming at the mouth! Clean him up and get him out of here."

I was taken into protective custody of imperial spies masquerading as invited guests of a prominent goldfish therapist, Dr. Foosiosy—a woman allegedly seen slow-dancing with a Venezuelan voting machine salesman at a birthday party for a leftist toad, Leaps Over Standing Corn (the same toad that pushed the firecracker down the throat of Sings Like A Bullfrog, "just to watch her explode.")

The spies strapped me to a hospital bed, covered me with glue, lemons, limes, oranges, and zzzzzzzzippypop. Then they blindfolded me, injected me with heroin and essential sleeping oils, suspended my bed from a hot-air balloon, and flew me to a secret location inside or outside the city.

I slept.

I woke up.

A woman in a lab coat with pixie-cut red hair and freckles stood over me. She looked familiar. Her eyes were green. Her vanilla perfume reminded me of Leslie.

"Are you Leslie?" I asked. "Did I kiss you sitting on a soft blanket in the flowers as we ate cherries and drank Coca-Cola on a spring day in fifth grade?"

"We removed your bladder," she said, ignoring the question. She pulled off her blood-spattered gloves. "We measured it, tried to bounce it, and put it back. It is sufficient, especially since you are catapult fodder. You will fight for the imperial resistance."

I inhaled through one nostril and exhaled out the other.

"In point of fact," she continued, "furthermore, moreover, and notwithstanding any prima facie pro bono defacto pleadings of starry decisis jurisdiction litigation, mediation consultation, solicitation mastication, or illumination of fossilized petrification in allegation flotation, Ms. Herein To Wit, the excellent legal assistant responsible for extracting notes from the meandering stream of consciousness of Lizard Fart Face, delivered a note to you from the Emperor just 13.46789 minutes ago, as follows:

Dear Stupid Idiot: Two days ago, Lizard Fart Face saw you fact-checking on your laptop, an offense indicating a preference for evidence and reality and, therefore, punishable by death. You are now alive only because Windy and I were in the middle of playing chutes and ladders when I learned of your treachery.

I am ordering you to the front, where you will suffer a painful death fighting the radical socialist crazies. Next time I see you, you'd better be dead, or some very bad things will happen to you ... *And don't even think* of telling your mother; she's resting up for another game. And if you think I'm just holding up a bible, you're very wrong and very stupid."

I felt myself losing all hope except for licorice ice cream and memories of Leslie. "This is a disappointing development."

The woman who examined my bladder said, "I can paraphrase the rest of the message. That might be easier for me."

Her red hair and freckles were irresistible. I looked directly into her green eyes. "Your vanilla perfume is perfect," I said.

"You are a big fat zero."

She paused, as if expecting me to respond, but I was mesmerized by her beauty.

"Wait," she said. She turned her head slightly and sneezed, showering my face with her precious bodily fluids. Could she be Leslie?

She wiped her face on her coat sleeve and examined the mucus. "Is there any snot on my face?"

"What?"

"Do I have snot on my face?"

"No, your face is clean as an orange popsicle, but mine is damp if that's any consolation."

"You are incompetent," she continued, "you have zero

charisma, no brains, no potential, zero women find you attractive, you are ugly, not handsome, wimpish, and your self-esteem is shot to hell. You have zero personality, you wet the bed until you were twelve, and your breath is bad."

I was falling in love.

"We are sending you to the front with 640 mules, catapults, cigars, cheap ballpoint pens, bows and arrows, and a letter for the commander."

"Will I see you again?"

She turned away and walked toward the door. I sensed she was weeping.

"At least your name!"

"I can't," she said without turning. "If you reject, my life would be over."

"You mean *defect*," I said.

"Whatever."

I TRAVELED to the front via a maze of underground tunnels, sixty five cubits x frichtoon gubenslaven. I rode atop a cynical Albino mule who claimed he was a Vietnamese prince and insisted I address him as "Sir Ten Lua Choi, Son of Rocket." We were followed by thirty-two teams of twenty brown mules, all of which would be dead within sixteen hours for reasons including gravitational pull. The mules pulled enormous catapults piled with instruments of death. I carried a letter for the commander.

A blue and green parrot who stood five feet tall when perched on a gray poodle belonging to a Ms. Dowager Cumberbun from Cincinnati announced our arrival. "A letter for the commander! Squawk! A letter for the commander!

Squawk! Squawk! A letter for the commander! A letter for the commander!" A letter for the commander!

Using its beak, the parrot took the reins of the Albino mule-prince and led us to a medical tent where four experienced rodent-exterminators injected me with confusion, amnesia, non-sequiturs, and LSD.

The ghost of Rush Limbaugh guided me to a briefing in the shade of a butternut tree in front of a modest, inanimate house in the country. Imperial fighters smoking fat cigars lingered in groups. Catapults surrounded by mules dotted the grass-covered hills.

The commander spoke to five, ten, or twenty officers seated in glowing yellow recliners in a semicircle around her. "Radical Socialists have overrun the city and are now advancing into the suburbs with scented candles, facts, heroin, strong body odor, and poor taste in shoes. They recruit rodeo clowns, tree huggers, goons, refugees, flying tuna fish, suicidal kangaroos, and rabid ostriches."

The yellow and orange sunset swirled behind her. She had red hair in a pixie cut, freckles, and green eyes. She wore camouflage fatigues. She appeared familiar. She looked at me. Her eyes were luminescent, bright, penetrating.

"I have many muuuuuuulessssss," I said, or thought I said, in a slow, delayed wave of soft ice-cream curling gently downward into a sugar cone, "and bows and arrowsssss, catapults not a few, and this letter for the commanderrrrrrr." I lifted the envelope into the air, holding it with my fingers attached to my hand attached to my arm, rotating upward from my shoulder like a fleshy crane hoisting a flat, alien spaceship. "Is time running out or short somewhere else?"

"Time is an atomic clock in Switzerland where people yodel and wear funny little short pants with suspenders," she said. "I am the commander." Her green eyes morphed into glittering emeralds. She patted the spot next to her on a swinging loveseat. "Come, sit here. Bring me the letter." Her voice bubbled, her face and hair a speckled comet trailing flames.

I moved my body toward hers, stepping on the undulating grass in slow, deliberate flotation. Her emerald eyes remained in contact with mine, seeing all, reading my thoughts, unzipping my skin. I sat next to her. She wore vanilla perfume.

The eyes of the officers seated in the recliners formed a semicircle of vibrating jealousy around us. The house behind them had faded white siding, a black roof, windows framed in red, white, and blue.

"Do you like the fenestration?" she asked me.

"I don't know. I'm not sure ... Fenestration? Is it related to that excellent case study, *Thought Fragmentation and Inner Turmoil in a Psychotic Rubix Cube?* Fenestration rhymes with fragmentation, and, it seems to me, could be related to the confusion of time zones by disorganized Rubix Cubes attached to satellites in space. The glue ap—"

"Never mind!" she said, "I was talking about the window frame, but it's not important." She laid her head on my shoulder.

The officers shifted nervously in their recliners. Two lit cigars. One removed his shirt and flexed his muscles. "I do her pedicures," he said, looking at me, obviously trying to intimidate. I laughed nervously and slid a few inches away from the commander. She grabbed the side of my shirt and tugged me back.

"I need you," she whispered.

Testosterone surged through my body. I imagined myself standing, pulling her into my arms. She, responsive, supple as rubber toothpick; me lost in her emerald eyes, kissing her passionately.

"I could do your pedicures," I said.

She seemed undecided, unsure, hesitant.

"Do I look familiar?" she asked.

"You do. Perhaps we met at one time or another, or maybe not. You smell like Leslie."

"I once held your bladder in my hands," she said, "and tried to bounce it."

"Okay," I said. I was surprised, even taken aback. "I don't recall that specific incident, but I may have amnesia, plus my memory's not so good." It all sounded a little far-fetched for publication in medical journals or Dr. Seuss. But she was beautiful, and if anyone was going to bounce my bladder, I wanted it to be her.

Dark silhouettes of migrating geese flew in the shimmering orange and yellow sunset.

A fully clothed woman in magenta scrubs approached and spoke to the commander, "The prisoner is ready for interrogation."

"Very well," the commander said, turning to me. "You will assist."

The commander and I entered the house. The interior was littered with cheap ballpoint pens, broken arrows, cigarettes, beer cans, syringes, poorly written memos, and moldy cheese. The prisoner was gagged and strapped to a bed. He was no more than twenty or twenty-five or thirty-five years old. His hair was brown or blond, dirty or clean.

The woman in magenta scrubs stood near the prisoner. She introduced herself.

"I'm Hulga," she said. "Head nurse for torture, executions, and quality assurance." She handed the commander a lab coat.

The lab coat immediately stiffened and threatened to play cards until midnight if stains and working-class fabrics were not given proper representation in labor negotiations.

Apparently trying to keep the peace, the commander put the lab coat on with a degree of respect uncommon for doctors who are generally associated with the upper-middle-class and have little in common with the midwifery practiced in clothing reproduction, especially in such distant locations as India, Sri Lanka, Vietnam, and ǐrú tā zùijìn zài xiānggǎng bèibǔn.

The commander smiled at me. I fell deeper in love, wanting my face close to hers, almost touching.

"I am a physician," she said.

I was transported back to fifth grade and a time by the river, when, intoxicated by Leslie's Vanilla perfume and green eyes, I suggested we play doctor, with me as the doctor, but she said no.

The commander had Hulga remove the gag from the prisoner and addressed him, "Are you insane, or do you have a full bladder?"

"NO!" he said, then he spit at the commander and spewed an impressive range of profanity. Hulga gagged him.

The commander removed the lab coat and put it on a hanger, then gave it her full attention. "You have yet to endure hardship, my long-sleeved friend, other than occasional splatters of blood, vomit, excrement, and periodic drowning in bleached waters at temperatures less than boiling. I could change all that." The lab coat adjusted itself on the hanger, appeared to bristle with hatred and screamed "CAPITALIST SCUM!!!!" so loud that everyone jumped. The coat then laughed derisively at upper-class dust mites in the room and addressed the commander, "I have no fear of you or your pompous assertions of superiority based on being made in the image of the creator!"

The commander calmly took the lab coat off the hook and quickly put it under her feet. It attempted to squirm its way out from under her, but she stood firm. She explained to the humans, rodents, dust mites, and bacteria within earshot that positioning the lab coat under her feet was to prevent a general rebellion among local items of clothing, many of which were created in locations influenced by unions, strikes, and dissatisfied cowboy boots.

"The lab coat," the commander said, "has a strong personality. I'll just leave it at that for now and deal with it in my own way when the interrogation of the radical socialist is completed." She traded a conspiratorial glance with Hulga, who stepped on the lab coat's collar with her left heel and leveraged all her considerable weight, grinding her foot into the garment while sharing a smile with the rest of us.

"But I digress," the commander said, looking at me. "The prisoner has been electrocuted and injected with psilocybin and substances that cannot be mentioned in mixed company." She then looked deep into my eyes and took a deep breath. "Are you familiar with the junior league of Sacramento?"

"I can't be sure," I said. "It sounds familiar, but I don't know … Life can be hard sometimes, and some wonder if we are alone in the universe, destined to absolute zero after this life except for inside the digestive tracts of unusual worms. On the other hand, maybe we're not flat or round characters, but some combination of Junior League and Rotary Club. Yet Sacramento is relatively close. It's a conundrum. I can't be sure."

The commander hesitated, then appeared to come to a decision, reconciled to uncertainty. "The prisoner will talk if we bend his fingers back vigorously and pull out his hair with these unusual tweezers." She handed me the unusual tweezers. "Okay, now pull his hair out with the unusual tweezers while I break his fingers and do the interrogation."

In the end, several clumps of bloody hair were deposited in a rectangular container of shallow depth. Six fingers were broken. The prisoner, a radical socialist from Wisconsin, made gagged attempts to spew profanities between screams and calling for his mother.

He finally gave up. The commander removed the gag. He admitted guilt and confirmed that the radical socialists and their recruits, rodeo clowns, immigrants, goons, flying tuna fish, suicidal kangaroos, and rabid ostriches were planning an attack.

He said the enemy's weapons were positioned with the intent of complete annihilation of the imperial resistance, children, rodents, and bank loan applications. "Expect the attack sooner rather than later," he said.

The commander wept. I wanted desperately to hold her in my arms and comfort her but contented myself with vomiting into a nearby waste basket. Hulga cut herself several times and requested psychiatric leave.

AT DUSK, a radical socialist airship, an immense blimp—and I mean really big, ominous, sinister, threatening, menacing, inauspicious, gloomy, and eerie looking—floated in from the west, eclipsing light. I checked the freezer for ice cream and asked a child if there was some place to hide. The commander found me in the cellar with children, old women, a blind man, a carton of fudge ripple.

"I was checking on the children and the old women and the blind," I said. "Here, I brought you all ice cream. You will have to share the spoon."

"Will you fiddle as Rome burns?" the commander asked me.

"Do you have a fiddle?"

Wrong thing to say. She was boiling. "You are a candy-pants, ice cream sucking coward. Go get a bow, arrows, an assortment of cheap ballpoint pens, and a whistle. Climb an assiduous tree behind the house and find a branch to sit on."

"You mean *deciduous* tree," I said.

"Whatever! ... Blow the whistle if you see the enemy. You will hold the line and fight to the death if necessary."

"I was just about to do that anyway."

Rats!

I climbed a tree that offered good cover. It was dark out

except for our patriot searchlights crisscrossing the sky, revealing the black underbelly of the blimp.

At intervals, one or more of our catapults could be heard springing, hurling mules high into the night sky where they tumbled through the searchlights before plunging to their deaths, their spirits bouncing from their bodies into eternal pastures of sunshine and clover.

"War is hell," I said to my imaginary friend Tim.

The bottom of the airship opened with a tremendous crash not unlike the sound of inanimate objects of heavy and immense proportions crashing open. Searchlights revealed huge vats rotating to an upside-down position, dumping liquid that covered everything on the ground with a yellow, glowing substance of unknown chemical composition combined with urine and chicken noodle soup.

My tree was spared. I inhaled deeply through one nostril and exhaled out the other.

The commander was nowhere to be seen. "Perhaps we should go back to the cellar," Tim suggested, but it was too late. The ground offensive was upon us. Radical socialist tree huggers, laughing maniacally, used catapults made of hardened tofu to launch blazing chunks of coal soaked in crude oil and gasoline at us, lighting up the sky, raining death and destruction down upon our forces like an ironic nightmare.

Enemy parachutes dropped from the blimp, landing armed rodeo clowns, suicidal kangaroos, immigrants, rabid ostriches, heroin, forged resumes, and flying tuna fish.

I soiled my pants and dropped the whistle to the ground.

"Pretend you're part of the tree!" Tim ordered.

I wrapped myself around the trunk like a pressed flower camouflaged as bark.

I whispered affirmations to draw upon the powers of the universe. "I am invisible. No one can see me. I look like tree bark. I am one with the tree. The tree loves and protects me."

A fire erupted in my right buttock. I looked down. A long arrow, with the exception of the tip, which was lodged securely in my butt, hung from my body. Its point of origin appeared to be the rodeo clown standing on the ground beneath me, affixing another arrow to his bow.

"I surrender!" I yelled.

Something huge crashed above me with an explosion of branches and leaves, and a mule slammed toward the earth, demolishing branches all around me and landed squarely on the rodeo clown below, crushing and covering all of him except one foot in a cheap cowboy boot protruding from under the dead mule's belly.

"You fool!" I exclaimed triumphantly. "Next time, buy alligator!"

My attention was at that very moment wrenched back to my inflamed buttock and the arrow hanging from it. "I'm out of here," I told Tim. I shimmied gently as possible down the tree, trying to avoid bumping the offending arrow on parts of the tree not destroyed by the mule. I simultaneously kept watch for hostile mammals, fish, birds, rodents, rodeo clowns, radical socialists, etc. The cacophony of battle continued around me. I trembled.

I reached the ground and asked the universe and any unaffiliated cosmic beings to assist me in finding painless solutions for removing the arrow and surviving the battle. "Find heroin," Tim said. "Hide under a dead mule." My butt was exploding with pain.

Suddenly, as if in answer to my celestial supplication, I smelled Leslie's perfume and turned around to find the commander gazing at me. Her freckled face was smeared with dirt, but she remained stunningly beautiful. She carried a bow and had a quiver of arrows strapped to her back. A number of cheap ballpoint pens, some bloody, rested in a plastic pocket protector near her right breast.

"Are you alright?" she asked.

"Yes," I said ... searching for exactly the right words. "But I had to throw a mule on this rodeo-clown leech-maggot who shot me in the butt with a projectile." I pointed at his boot. "Before that, I shot all my arrows to deadly effect, sometimes killing three radical socialists with one shot. I then used my bow to bludgeon a suicidal kangaroo to death and fend off a rabid ostrich. I gouged out the eyes of a refugee with my cheap ballpoint pens, strangled a flying tuna fish, tripped a goon as he ran by, and beat him to death with my bare hands. I was about to come rescue you from imminent danger."

"Impressive," she said. "Unfortunately, the battle is not going our way in other locations up, down, or sideways. The mules are all dead, as are many fighters, top-ranking officers, and thirty-six lawmakers, snuffed out while gesticulating wildly, spitting and drooling in anger at proposed taxes on private jets parked illegally in Guadalajara.

I've decided to surrender to spare the lives of the remaining patriots, rodents, stockbrokers named Rosalyn, and banking executives with mental disorders who agree to tonsillectomies. I want you to be with me when I surrender ... I love you." She smiled.

Oh, my heart. My testosterone! "I love you too," I said. I took her supple and willing body in my arms, bent her backward, and kissed her passionately.

"I am Leslie," she whispered, her arms around my neck, her face close to mine. "I've dreamt of finding you since that spring day in fifth grade, the day we kissed on the soft blanket near the river, surrounded by flowers."

THE SURRENDER WAS HUMILIATING, perhaps, or maybe not so much, depending on your point of view and the fact you were not there. A squat, painted rodeo clown who juggled oranges, lemons, and watermelons injected me with heroin and a mixture of essential oils before yanking the bloody arrowhead out of my butt.

Leslie and I were paraded through the suburbs and the city in an aquarium drained of water and mounted on a wagon. The wagon was pulled by captured rodents and an alligator found chewing on the right leg of a goon in the shallow end of an oval-shaped blue swimming pool behind a 3,600 square-foot stucco home rented by three lively dwarves with excellent resumes printed on cardstock.

We were tried by a military tribunal consisting of radical socialists, brightly colored parrots raised by Benedictine monks, tricycles, the Amazonian rainforest, and cheap postcards.

Horned owls and discount coupons were called as witnesses.

We were sentenced to death and spent six months in adjacent cells on death row surrounded by fellow members of the patriot resistance, prominent capitalists, a family of field mice swept up in a general purging of suspected republicans, and two executives, identical twins, arrested by secret police for wearing matching silk ties while purchasing hot dogs from a street vendor in Boise.

The evening before our scheduled execution, just last night, Leslie was granted her request for a small bottle of the vanilla perfume she wore the day we kissed in fifth grade. She put it on, and we held hands through the night.

She was scheduled to die at 7:00 a.m. and me at 8:00 a.m.

As they came down the row to take her, she squeezed my hand and looked at me with those amazing green eyes. "Death by guillotine is painless."

"Yes," I said, "yes, yes, yes. And I love you. And I always will. You are everything to me."

Then they took her, and when she disappeared through the door at the end of the row, I sat down and wondered aloud, "How could she possibly know that? How could anyone know that ...?"

Here they come.

And that was all he wrote.

AUTONOMY HIGH

CALLIE STOKER

Contemporary Science Fiction/Superheroes

Chapter 1

"*W*hat are you wearing, Mr. E?" Danni lowered the book she was reading at her desk and pointed at my jacket, her disbelief getting the attention of the whole class.

Even Noah put down the mess of wires he'd been constructing into some cube shape, then pushed up his glasses. "Yeah, man. What's up with the Tweedy Professor?"

I tried not to feel too offended by a kid who fit every stereotype of "nerd" himself, but hey, Noah can make anything from motors to motherboards out of dumpster finds, so he's earned the title in the best of ways.

I stowed my bag under my desk, which faced the six kids who sat at two long tables, making up two rows of KPAs—Kids Possessing Abilities—here at Autonomy High. The bell had rung a few minutes ago, and I'd chosen an important topic for class today, but perhaps they needed a little banter before jumping into philosophy.

As an APA teacher (Adult Possessing Abilities—I know, the big-wigs really stretched their minds on these classifications), I breathed in the field-of-flowers scent that filled the room and let my ability tell me that everyone was in a pretty good mood. Razzing your teacher will do that.

"Are you leaving us, *professor?*" Dev sped into class in a blink and now joined in on the daily roast, looking to the others to see their reactions. You'd think a kid with super speed would never be late. "Going to join the *big-league* college bros?"

"Now we gotta call him professor, don't we?" Danni closed her book-of-the-day, which looked to be on stargazing, then leaned back to high-five Dev.

I raised my hands in an attempt to quiet them down, laughing along. I mean, I *had* chosen tweed this morning, so I really should have seen this coming. I put on my snobbiest of accents: "That's right. Call me Professor Evan Longstone." Drawing out the "stooowne."

Laughs and groans morphed the room's scent to candy-sweet amusement, mixed with the ever-present high-school reality of teen body odor.

"For today, I will be impressing (I rolled the crap out of that "r") upon your minds a question of deep psychological interest." A pause for dramatic effect. "What forms a man? His nature? Or his nurture?"

"Well, there he goes ..." Danni waved a resigned hand and settled deeply into her seat while the rest of the class sent me good-natured eyerolls. The scent in the room dampened but didn't turn, so I think I managed the segue into our topic pretty well.

Danni folded her arms in a kind of "impress me" challenge. Keeping her interested took a different type of teaching. She could memorize facts so easily that focusing on dates and data points didn't keep her brain alert or active. Honestly, good memory or not, that kind of teaching didn't keep *any* kids interested.

The students settled back into their chairs, all except Spencer, who very rarely stayed in his seat.

"Teach on, Mr. E." He floated in kind of a cross-legged seating position behind the back row. Flying may be the ability everyone wishes for, but all I know is fliers sure hate to sit still.

I pointed at the words I'd written on the smart board behind me: Nature vs. Nurture.

The flavor in the room muted to a kind of woodsy, grassy smell. I categorized all nature-related odors as a kind of peaceful acceptance. If the scent turned moldy, I would know they'd moved to boredom, and I'd need to change tactics to wake them back up.

"Both have significant impact on who a person will be. But which influences make the greater difference?"

The smart board was controlled by the tablet on my desk. I picked it up, ready to type out class responses. I can't tell you how jealous I am of telekinetic APAs who can do all of this with just their brains.

Danni's head popped up at the question. I could almost see the ideas churning in her mind.

Noah's hands worked faster on his little objects, something I'd learned meant his brain was working just as fast. Even Spencer's hand shot up.

The room filled with the blooming scent of growing minds.

Chapter 2

DISCUSSION FINISHED, the smart board was now filled with long lists of what influences form who we become. I asked them to write or draw or type out their final feelings (depending on how they expressed themselves best) when a small knock at our door was followed by Mrs. Trent, the superintendent. That woman could talk anyone into anything—literally—and once again, I was grateful that I couldn't smell my own emotions as my anxiety rose at the possibility of being roped into some school function or fundraiser. Or maybe she was here to make some kind of announcement to the kids that another villain had been captured by the SDF. They seemed to find a new one every day.

Mrs. Trent's heels clacked as she walked toward me. Her hair was pinned up, and the hot pink cardigan she wore over a colorful skirt begged that we see her as "approachable." But she didn't have to try so hard. We all respected Mrs. Trent. She nearly always smelled calmly of that fresh nature smell you get after it rains.

A student in a yellow hoodie followed hesitantly behind her.

Mrs. Trent waved her into the class. "Miss Elloy. Come in— if you choose?" Mrs. Trent was always very careful with her words.

The new girl moved further into the classroom, and an acrid scent surrounding her told me she'd rather be anywhere else.

The kids dutifully sat up a bit. Spencer sank down into a seat in the back row as if to claim it before the new girl could.

"Class, I'd like you to meet Kaz Elloy. She's a new student here at Autonomy High School, and I *hope* you'll all welcome her and help her adjust to her new surroundings."

Everyone listened when she spoke—even when she didn't demand it with her ability, which in my memory, she never had.

At least half the class gave little nods.

"Wonderful!" Mrs. Trent turned brightly on her heels and left, giving me a quick look before leaving. And she was leaving quickly, as if she didn't want me to catch the citrusy tang of lime overlaying her natural scent. Citrusy scents are categorized under hiding something. I'd have to ask her about that later.

146

I got up from my desk and offered a fist bump to Kaz. Because I'm cool like that.

She looked a little skeptical but bumped back.

I pointed to an open seat in the center, second row, next to the territorial Spencer.

Danni gave her a big smile from the front row, and Dev nodded a bit as Kaz sank into the chair between him and Spencer.

Spencer kept eye contact with her as he let go of his chair and floated back up to his customary spot between desk and ceiling.

Kaz didn't react; instead, she put her head down on the desk.

I sat back at my desk, giving the kids a few more minutes on their responses, when a dizzy sickness flashed through me, quick as lightning. A metallic smell— an uncategorized odor—singed my nose, short-circuiting my thoughts. I gripped my head as an image formed. A dark room. A person—someone familiar—was looking down at me, but they were only a silhouette, back-lit by a bluish light.

"Mr. E., you good?" Dev was beside me with a gust that shifted the papers on my desk.

I tried to nod, waving him away that all was fine. But that smell, it had triggered something that felt real. I had gaps in my past, a common thing for an orphaned kid who had grown up in survival mode. And I'd had enough therapists congratulate me for not dwelling on past things that I hadn't spent much time worrying about how I barely remembered my mother and had no information about my father.

That face, only an impression of a face, really, was one of them, I was sure of it, and I needed to know more.

With my eyes still closed, a different smell distracted me. It was Suni's sweet perfume, and her quiet voice sounded worried as she joined Dev at my desk. "Should I ... should I run to the office?" Suni, seated invisibly next to Danni in the front row, was often quiet, and I was grateful at least that my sensitive nose could detect her presence, perhaps a bit easier than another APA teacher would. Another powerful ability, but it had its drawbacks.

"Yeah, man. You don't look too good." Chet was in the front row, and the desk creaked unnaturally as he leaned forward. He was a little sensitive about his strength and how often things broke around him, so I didn't say anything.

The scent of decay was edging around their natural odors, classic fear category. I needed to snap out of it.

The new kid Kaz looked around, confused.

I got up and waved them to their seats. "I'm fine. Sorry, guys. Just got dizzy."

Dev and Suni sat back down, but the rotten stench remained.

"I think my blood sugar is low or something." I tried infusing some energy into the words, so my weird behavior had some believable excuse.

They all just looked at me. I'd really scared them.

Kaz was still in her seat, gauging the other's reactions, probably thinking she'd hit the jackpot of weirdo teachers.

I rummaged through a drawer and pulled out a fun-size Snickers that had probably been there since Halloween and held it up. "I'm good. I'll be fine."

Most of them nodded and went back to their work.

Danni took the longest to stop staring; I don't think I'd convinced her. But then she turned around to whisper some instructions to Kaz about what everyone was working on and offered her a piece of paper, for which I was grateful.

I unwrapped the candy bar and ignored the thin layer of oxidation as I chewed and swallowed. Darkly sweet, salty peanuts. The taste nearly obliterated the memory of that awful smell that had hit me.

Likewise, the room returned to its neutral leafy scent. Still, a part of me wanted to trigger that metallic aroma again, just to see more of that dark room. That face.

"Done." Danni was at my desk, handing me several pages of writing. She always preferred handwriting her work rather than typing it. Her hand reeked of something damp and disintegrating, so I didn't need to see her eyes to know she was still worried for me.

"Feeling better already." I smiled my best reassuring smile and crumpled up the tiny candy bar wrapper, tossing it in the nearby trash.

Chapter 3

AFTER THE PRESENTATIONS OF THE KIDS' papers, with arguments comparing therapeutic correctional hospitals vs. jail cells or artwork filled with cradled babies vs. babies left in playpens, the bell rang, and the clatter of kids gathering their bags and papers began.

"Remember our essay quiz tomorrow!" I shouted over the squeaks of chairs and desks.

"Bye, Mr. E." Suni wafted by me.

"Yeah, bye." Danni was back to her sweet, cheery mood, which put a smile on my face. I gave them both a little wave.

Noah, shoving his bits and bobs into his pockets, was usually the last one out the door, so I busied myself with collecting my own stacks of papers and rehearsing how best to introduce tomorrow's quiz topic.

"Uh ... Mr.—?"

I looked up to find Kaz in front of me. She had startlingly light eyes, almost like clear glass, that peeked from beneath her oversized yellow hoodie.

"It's Mr. Lockstone." I pointed at myself, forcing my brain

not to focus on the putrid emotional smells coming off her, dripping with anxiety. I understood. I'd been a new kid too.

"Or Mr. E. My first name's Evan." I was clearly overexplaining.

She nodded. "Okay. Mr. E." She held out a piece of paper. "I wrote this, but if I did it wrong ..."

I took it, a little surprised. She'd joined us after the discussion, so I figured she'd just listen in to the other's presentations. A prick of shame hit me. I'd let that stupid smell, that memory or whatever, really distract me. I should have clarified, or at least checked in with her.

"No, no. Anything is great. I like to hear everyone's thoughts." I looked down at the page. It looked neatly written, and I found myself excited to read it.

I didn't know what ability she had, but her willingness to jump right into the work was refreshing. So many kids came to our school from unsafe conditions, and it took months, sometimes longer, to see them come out of their shell.

"This is great, Kaz. Thank you. Do you need help finding the cafeteria?"

She shook her head and turned to go, her hood still covering most of her face.

I SPENT my evening looking over the students' notes and drawings. Wonderful expressions of the way they saw the world and themselves. Were we the jumbled set of our circumstances? Most of the kids in my class had long lists of unfairnesses they'd dealt with in life, but the consensus seemed to be that it was more complicated than a comparative list of nature biology and nurture influences.

Kaz had written what I'd consider a full essay. She focused

on the dangers of control as less nurture and more manipulation and that a living being needed freedom and choice to thrive. I had to agree and wondered what her life experiences had been to teach her this at her age.

After a hurried meal of leftover Kung Pao and fried rice, I allowed myself a quick glance at the news feeds. A villain with earth manipulation had been captured today, and two other ADAs had warrants out for immediate arrest due to unlawful ability use.

The SPF had enough ADAs that I wasn't overly worried. The balance of power was pretty firmly on the "good" side, but it was still news that made my bones itch. I didn't want to imagine a world where that balance shifted.

I shut off the news feed, but before turning in, I pulled out a box of old photos from behind my closet. Perhaps I could pick out the face from that sudden memory that had hit me today.

I had long ago dealt with my past, being an orphan pulled from my dead mother's home, taken in by a nice family living in Special Defense Force housing. They'd sat me down and explained how my mother was gone now, and I could call them Mom and Dad if I wanted to.

I flipped through photos of the obligatory birthday poses, the day I graduated from college, flanked by Henry's broad-shouldered form and Tracy's kind smile. They'd been good parents, and I was grateful for them.

Looking back at it now, it should be shocking how easily I'd moved on. But that was the way of trauma, wasn't it? I remembered so little of my life before coming here. I hadn't thought of my mother's face ... maybe ever. I could recall that her eyes had been dark like mine, her hair wild and full around her head, and I was suddenly convinced that the familiarity I'd felt in that triggered memory, that face looking down on me, was her.

But sitting in my room, I couldn't grab on to anything else, no childhood memory of her, not even a happy one. I had no photos of her, no more clues, so I pushed those thoughts back and went to bed, though I spent most of the night in tortured review of that glimpse of her silhouette, moonlit by those windows in that otherwise dark room.

Chapter 4

WHEN THE BELL RANG, I'd just finished writing up the day's question for our quiz on the smart board.

Most of the kids were in or near their seats as I turned around to face them, filling the room with their various aromas. I was pleased to see Kaz in the same spot she'd chosen yesterday, chatting with Danni sitting in front of her.

"You have a wild night, Mr. E?" Spencer said, at least two feet from his actual seat. His tone was teasing, but it got the others to look up at me.

Before I could reply, Danni jumped in. "Yeah, Mr. E, you sick?"

"I'm fine, guys. Just had a bad night's sleep." To change the subject, I pointed back at the board. "Now, let's focus up. Today's our essay quiz. This counts for a quarter of your grade because we only do four of these each year."

I could feel their interest wane significantly as the room turned moldy. I hadn't done as a good a job of transitioning us today, my head was still fuzzy from tossing all night. But deep (deep) down, they didn't totally hate this way of proving they'd learned something this quarter. We didn't do standardized testing here. Our school was built by Special Defense Forces (SPD), open only to KWAs, and most of the teachers were APAs (Adults Possessing Abilities) like myself. The people in charge wanted to develop heroes, not future villains, so there was a big emphasis on the discussion of philosophy, ethics, history, and culture, and these subjects were tested best by discussion, debate, in written or artistic expression, not multiple choice.

I glanced at the clock. "You have an hour to write out your thoughts." I pointed back at the smart board. What Does "Free to Choose" Mean to You? Remember to use the points and research we've been collecting all quarter to support your conclusions." I sat at my desk, pulling out the rest of yesterday's work to give feedback and enter into my tablet.

The nervous smell of decay hovered around me, and I saw Kaz standing at my desk. Of course, she wouldn't be familiar with our procedures, and I'd just left her hanging there.

"Kaz. You could probably use a few more instructions, huh?" I smiled but couldn't quite catch her eyes, still hidden under her yellow hood. "Come with me."

We left the classroom and passed Noah, who preferred to do his writing in the hall, to cut down distractions. I could see he was writing something about "childhood trauma." He knew a few things about that; his dad was a bastard, and if the man wasn't currently in jail, Noah may have quite literally killed him with some homemade gadget or other. This school and the nearby community had provided him and his mom a refuge, and I was grateful to see how he'd blossomed over the last few years.

Kaz followed me down the hall, past two other classrooms with quiet noises of discussion or study and smells that matched. We turned right, and I led her into the media room. Here, she might feel a bit more comfortable, and I could give her some instructions without bothering the others.

Mrs. Lu looked up from her usual spot behind the desk and gave a little nod, acknowledging the presence of teacher and student. She'd been the librarian here when I was a kid, and although she didn't believe in favoritism, I knew she liked it when I stopped by to share a book recommendation or ask how her grandkids were doing. If I was lucky, she would even stretch her long arms around me for a quick squeeze.

We sat at one of the long tables near a half-bookcase of colorful spines with fantasy titles.

"I'm sure you're a little confused," I started, hoping to help her feel more comfortable.

She shrugged as she slid into the plastic chair.

"Being the new student kinda sucks."

Another shrug. Now wasn't the time for personal sharing. We could "relate" later.

"Well, today, the kids are sharing their viewpoints on all the discussions we've been having the last several weeks. You caught the end of yesterday's discussion, the one about nature vs. nurture?"

She nodded beneath her hood.

"Okay, well, I read over the essay you gave me yesterday. I don't know if you meant for it to be an essay, but it was really well presented. I'm impressed."

I paused for a reaction, but she stayed silent.

"It was well thought out. I especially liked your points about choices and manipulation. It actually inspired today's question."

More silence. That was fine. I plowed on.

"So, in my opinion, for as little of the discussion you heard, and the fact that you are new, I don't think you need to do much else. I'm happy to count your writing yesterday toward today's quiz and, in my opinion, you aced it."

Kaz looked up sharply, and again I saw the strikingly clear color of her eyes. "I don't want to be given any favors. I'm new, not stupid."

"No, no." I raised two hands. "Of course not. I'm not trying to imply—"

"Just give me the quiz, and I'll do it." Her hood overtook her eyes again as she looked down. There wasn't a lot of heat behind her words, but there was a tinge of annoyance and the clear tinge of vinegar, the quietest hint of anger.

I sat back. It made sense. She didn't want to be treated differently. Being "othered" was a trigger for a lot of kids who came here for a variety of reasons. But it wasn't fair to make her write on subjects she'd missed entirely. Maybe if she wrote about something she knew? Cared about? "Okay, I hear you. From what I saw yesterday, it looks like you are a good writer. Or at least, pretty comfortable with writing?"

We were back to shrugs for responses. Yet she'd spoken up for herself. That was impressive.

"How about you write about what you know? Something important to you."

She lifted her face, mouth opening to argue, but I stopped her.

"I know that sounds like I'm treating you differently or coddling you or whatever. I swear I'm not. I'll apply the same level of critique to your work that I do theirs, but you haven't sat in on our discussions, so unless you want to write another wonderful essay about freedom of choice, I suggest we go with something you already know. Fair?"

She shut her mouth, those clear eyes considering. Then she nodded sharply and relaxed a bit in the squeaky chair. "Okay. What subject?"

"That's up to you." I tried to look more relaxed, too, although I had to admit my crappy night of sleep was getting to me. I needed some caffeine. "I always find it easy to write about something I care about. How about what brought you here to us? Or what your life was like before—"

"I don't want to talk about that." Tangy vinegar misted the air between us.

"That's fine. That was just one idea." I softened my voice, leaning forward a bit.

Mrs. Lu was in the back corner now, long arms stretching seven feet or so to shelve a book.

"Writing is about saying something. So ... what do you have to say?"

"To you?" She looked incredulous.

I cracked a smile. "To the world."

Chapter 5

I LEFT Kaz in the media center with a school laptop and instructions on what time to come back to class. She'd already opened it and started typing before I left, so something had sparked an idea in her. I was excited to see what it would be.

Back in the classroom, the kids were bent over papers, journals, and laptops. Many had piles of the writing and drawings from earlier discussions as references for their essays today. Noah was still writing as I'd passed him in the hall.

Thirty more minutes of time before I'd have them wrap things up.

I gulped a Diet Coke from a stash behind my desk and opened my own computer, feeling pretty good about how I'd worked things out with Kaz.

Just as I relaxed into the momentary lull, that metallic smell hit again. So powerful, I leaned forward, gripping my desk. Inside my head felt like a thousand sparks lighting up.

I bit down on my lip, desperate to stay silent but also needing to allow this.

As expected, my mind filled with the dark room I'd been seeing. I was there now, viewing it from a low point, like a child looking up, seeing two long windows covered in paper shades. It was dark outside, but the moonlight backlit the image of the woman above me. My mother. I knew it now. Her eyes were fierce, she was looking at me intensely, and I was afraid. Not of her, but of what was happening.

The electrical rush that accompanied the smell ran down my spine and, too quickly, the picture faded. I clawed to bring it back, to follow the silhouette of my mother's features, to try and understand why she looked so angry. Afraid? I couldn't pull any other smell from the memory outside that electrical scent, but this memory was important. Did it reveal how she had died?

"Mr. E?" Danni was at my desk.

I looked up, her musty, earthy scent pushing away the metallic one that kept assaulting me. Her scent wasn't worried, just a little confused. She pointed at the clock, journal in hand like she was ready to turn it in. "I think time's up."

She was right. I stood, part of me still locked in the room with my mother, but knowing I didn't have time to investigate any more of it. "Turn in your pages, or email them if you typed it." I pointed to my email posted at the front of the classroom, even though they all knew it by now.

A second later, Kaz walked in with the borrowed laptop, handing it out to me. I pointed to my email address, and she nodded and went to her desk to send the file to me. Noah followed her, handing in his own papers.

"Thanks for your hard work. You guys were really focused." Determined to pull out of my funk, I went full cheesy teacher mode and rubbed my hands together like some kind of crafty wizard. "I'm excited to see what you have in store for me!"

The class dutifully groaned.

"Okay, well, we're a bit early, but I'm going to go ahead and send you down to the cafeteria for lunch. You deserve some extra free time."

Chairs and desks clattered and squeaked as they did not hesitate to escape the classroom, already talking about what they'd smelled from the cafeteria earlier that day. Clearly, everyone was hoping for pizza rather than Ms. Awkana's greasy lasagna.

Kaz and Danni left together, and I was pleased to see a possible friendship blossoming there.

I gathered the papers and put them in a folder to look over tonight. I was in desperate need of some coffee, and maybe a sandwich or something. But I was also itching to see what Kaz had written, so I opened my computer and found her email in the list. I tapped the computer impatiently, waiting for the file to load. As soon as it opened, I started to read.

You want me to talk about what I care about. Does it matter what I care about? Really? My life is a joke. I don't have a say. Y'all act like this school is some great place. Like I'll be understood. But let's be honest. I was forced to be here.

I stopped reading. Her honesty was unexpected but certainly not wrong. This was a school for "special kids," a term I hated. But maybe expressing this, letting it out, would do her some good.

Y'all just took me. My parents literally died, and you just came and took me away. No one is talking to me, saying anything, but I know the truth. I know I killed them. I know it. Y'all just—

My desk rattled as I stood. She killed her parents? The citrus smell from Mrs. Trent. She *had* been hiding something from me. Shakily, I forced myself to keep reading.

—want to control everything. But control doesn't help. Believe me. I've tried. So, you can send in your stupid soldier goons, take me away from my home, never let me see my parents— even their bodies—to say goodbye, then dump me in this wack school and call it good.

I blink. Her words are shocking, sure. KPA's all come to this school with stories, but this one, if it was true, was brutal. Soldiers breaking in had to have been the SDFs. I could almost see them dragging her away, her parents' bodies on the ground—

That electric, metallic smell overtakes me, stronger than I've breathed in before. I crash back down into my chair, no longer fully connected to my body as I'm pulled again into that room, the darkness outside, my moonlit mother. Something releases in my head, and the full scene immerses me stronger than any scent or odor has ever overrun my senses.

"They're coming." Mom's intense eyes are wide, and I smell the fear on her, the acrid musk covering one of the ever-changing smells that usually surround her.

I'm small, really young, and I don't understand as I look up at her. Noxious ammonia stings my nose, causing my eyes to tear up. I've never sensed such strong emotion before.

She keeps looking at the front door of our small apartment, then back at me, and her toxic scent is more complex than my young mind can categorize.

A banging shakes the room. "Debbie Meuller, this is the Special Defense Force. Please power down and remain calm."

Mom presses clenched fists to her eyes. "Leave us alone!" she screams, and I'm dizzy with the malodorous weight of fear erupting from her, a category I was familiar with. Memories fill me of months, maybe years, of living in this insect-filled one-room hole, barely enough food to fill a single cupboard, and a mom who carries such a deep weight of worry and fear it saturates her clothing, her hair, and makes it hard to remember the times when she didn't smell like decomposing refuse.

I reach up, scared, needing my mother as the loud banging continues.

The door bursts open, and the space is filled with the overlapping helmets and broad-shouldered armor of several soldiers, a big white SDF on each chest.

Mother lowers her hands. Her eyes are glowing red.

The man in front tilts his head to his shoulder, as if he's speaking into a communication device. "She's still powered up. Shields and armor to maximum."

Mother's scent has changed, and I know she regrets not grabbing me, keeping me near her. But she's also not able to look at me in case she loses control of the rising energy building behind her eyes.

"If you take me, what will happen to him?" she asks, still keeping a distance, but I can see the fight is leaving her, too many years of trying and losing.

"He'll be taken to our campus. There's a school for kids with abilities. They will know how to help him."

Mom waves a dismissive hand. "And how will you use his power, huh? Mine has been useless every damn day of my life, so why do you want him?"

And I remember how she used to do fun things with her power, like stare and blink to cut my grilled cheese with her amazing laser eyes or cut a makeshift raft from a floating log in the nearby lake for us to float and splash in. But her aim wasn't too good, and sometimes she hit the ground instead, making the sand turn into a smokey hole of curling glass.

The head soldier guy steps forward a little. Mom's eyes glow red, and she lifts a hand to her temple, something she does to try and hit her mark.

He lifts a hand. "Ma'am, you know the law. You are in violation of the Accordance Abilities Act. You know there is no tolerance for illegal use of an ability. Our cameras have caught every instance of theft over the last three months, with or without the use of your ability, and it is enough to criminally prosecute."

For the first time ever, our fridge had been full of milk and eggs and cheese these last few weeks. Our freezer even had ice cream. We built chocolate sundaes in cereal bowls last night, and I had wondered why we were celebrating with such a special treat.

She'd known they would come.

"We will take care of your son, but if you want to live a normal life with him, you have to come with us."

The scene dimmed, and I lowered my head onto my desk, but I'm able to finish the memory now. I can remember it all. She opened her eyes and red beams shot out, bursting the windows as the shield from one of the SDF's abilities deflected the lasers. A soldier grabbed me, putting something over my head as he pulled me from the room. I screamed, that electrical, metallic smell that had been triggering me the past two days filled the bag, clogging my sense of any other odor. Sure that they would kill her, it was the first and only time I had smelled my own emotions.

How could I have forgotten it? Why hadn't I reviewed this night again and again as I'd been forced into a new home, new family?

But I knew why. I'd been as angry as Kaz was now. This had all just happened to her. Still, the block in memory bothered me. It felt purposeful, something more than just trauma.

I closed my computer, a heavy weight settling. Could I have done more to help Mom? Even if I couldn't as a child, what about a year or two later? What about now? Was she even still alive, or had that fight ended everything for her? I'm ashamed that I don't know.

As I tried to think of someone I could ask, Mrs. Lu was at my door. Her stretchy arms extended from the doorway to grab me by the shoulder. "Evan! One of your students. The new one!" Her arms pulled at my jacket, lifting me up to follow the rest of her, which was already out the door.

Something wrong with the new student. Kaz?

I followed Mrs. Lu and her scent of sweet rotting fruit as we ran through the cafeteria to the double doors that led to the outside exercise area.

Kaz had a power, and the SDF saw her as a threat.

Tension reinvigorated my exhausted limbs at the thought of anyone getting hurt today.

Outside, basketball nets, sky ball for the fliers, and steel balls for the super strong littered a stretch of blacktop flanked by tall trees and an electrical fence beyond. We pushed through a crowd of kids, forming a circle around a girl in a yellow hoodie.

She was glowing.

"What happened?" I asked anyone who would tell me.

Dev was next to me in a burst. "Some kid was teasing her or something? I don't know. But she warned him about making her mad. Then, dude, she started glowing!" He pointed at the obvious as Kaz's light shone brighter.

I spotted Mrs. Trent in another one of her cardigan and skirt sets just a few feet from Kaz. She didn't break eye contact with Kaz as I ran up. "I've told the students to stay back, but I haven't told Kaz what to do yet."

She *told* them? Mrs. Trent? She almost never gave a direct order. Everything she said, the listener was compelled to obey.

"Kaz is dangerous, isn't she?"

Mrs. Trent gave me a sharp look, then the fresh scent of truth rippled from her. "I'm sorry. I didn't want to spoil her fresh start by telling you the details, but yes. The SDF pulled high-level radiation readings from her when they grabbed her from her home."

I know I killed them. I know it.

Damn. I pushed away the creeping memories of my own memories and shielded my eyes against the increasing light emanating from Kaz, her face fully hidden by the hood. I stepped forward.

"Mr. Lockstone—"

I paused, but Mrs. Trent didn't give any further orders. I gave her a look that I hoped communicated "trust me" and continued slowly over to Kaz.

As I got closer, I could smell every bit of fear coming off her.

"Hey." I stepped forward again. Now that I was close enough to speak quietly to her, I tried not to think of how many doses of radiation were currently hitting my cells. Gratefully, the school nurse here was particularly talented.

"I can see you're having a hard time, yeah?" It was a stupid comment, but better than asking if she was okay when she clearly wasn't.

Her glow remained steady.

I tried again. "I read your essay."

Kaz's hood lifted a bit, but her face remained covered.

Her glow faded, so I continued. "Not every page yet, but enough to get it."

She didn't move, but I could smell her emotions shift. Rotted garbage to ammonia. Her glow intensified. My words were making her angry.

The crowd around us gasped at the change, and I wondered if Mrs. Trent was going to evacuate everyone soon. This wasn't a great time for an audience. But she was focused on Kaz, and I realized she was preparing to order Kaz to "STOP" if things intensified any more.

Mrs. Lu also stood close, using her stretched arms to hold the kids back.

I raised my hands. "Wait, wait. Sorry, I misspoke. I'm not saying I 'get it.' I can't really understand; of course, I can't. That was stupid." I pulled in a breath. My own memories were still new to me, but I wasn't an idiot. I saw the parallels here, looking again at someone powerful, someone in crisis, wanting to help but unsure how. Still, my vantage point was different. I wasn't any more powerful than I had been as a child, but I had words now that I hadn't back then. And enough empathy for the loss of family that I might be able to connect with Kaz.

"My mom was like you."

Kaz's glow pulsed.

"She was powerful, and her power hurt people, I think. It was a long time ago, and I don't remember everything."

I glanced at Mrs. Trent, whose face showed surprise at what I was saying. Citrus leaked from her direction. She knew something about what I was saying, but that was a distraction I couldn't risk right now.

I stepped forward just a bit more. Kaz's fear was strong enough to make my eyes water at the acrid odor, another connection to my mother's last moments.

"She wanted to protect me, but she didn't know how to even help herself. Her feelings were big. Lots of overlapping insecurities. They overwhelmed her every day, and she didn't know what to do with them." My memories confirmed what I was saying. In some ways, Mom had helped form my early classifications of smells and emotions. Her moods, an ever-changing kaleidoscope of aromas, an unpredictable mess that I'd quickly learned to identify and label.

Another step forward, although when I got close enough to touch her, I didn't know what I would do. Embrace some radiation burns as I try to give her an encouraging hug?

Still, my words seemed to be having an effect. Her glow was softening, the stench of her emotions diluting into something less sour. Her hood still covered her eyes.

"I'm sorry about your parents." I said it so softly, probably only she and maybe someone with a hearing ability would be able to pick it out.

She raised her eyes to me, and I could see her clear irises

now glowed in a crystal shimmer. It was incredible, and I found myself mesmerized.

"You don't know what you're talking about," she whispered back.

I nodded. Slowly. Carefully. Her scent was changing, the intensity of her feelings still churning, but it was a cornucopia of confused smells, as if someone had thrown twenty air fresheners and some rotting leftovers into a bowl of bleach and asked me to sniff it.

I resisted analyzing each smell, cataloging her emotions, and forced myself to remember instead what I'd come to say.

"I *don't* really know what you've been through. You're right." I stopped inching forward. We were comfortably close now. I just needed her to hear me and feel our conversation could be private. Maybe if her glow decreased enough, Mrs. Trent would feel ready to tell the kids to leave.

Then something broke all the tension, and the mess of smells melded together into a single mildewed slog.

Kaz's glow went out like a snuffed candle, and she collapsed.

I looked to Mrs. Trent to see if she had said something, but she shook her head.

Then I heard broken, wrenching sobs.

I bent down, reaching out softly to touch Kaz's shoulders.

Mrs. Lu decided the show was over, and the kids were begrudgingly shooed from the scene.

Mrs. Trent stayed close, but her changed scent told me the tension had calmed down.

As I made contact with Kaz's shaking shoulders, she snapped out of her tears and sat up.

Mrs. Trent stiffened again, but by now, the kids and Mrs. Lu had left. The courtyard area was quiet as Mrs. Trent and I collectively held our breath to see what Kaz would do next.

"I'm not a victim," Kaz whispered harshly, but her glow didn't return, and her eyes were back to their clear, colorless shade, glaring at us from beneath the yellow hood as she remained huddled on the blacktop. "I'm the villain. Don't you get it?" Her scent was a different kind of anger now, more musty tang than acrid burn. It was the kind of anger that came with hurt.

I blinked away my watery eyes now that her scent had eased up, then relaxed my stance.

Mrs. Trent followed my lead, eyes still on Kaz.

"They think they can control me, get *me* to control my powers, but it's impossible. I'm just going to hurt people. Even when I don't want to." As her voice raised, I could see the first wisps of yellow light forming along her hands, her eyes lighting up again.

A sour pit formed in my stomach. Her words were tugging at emotional memories. Crying in a dirty apartment because there wasn't any food in the kitchen. Mom pulling granola bars and half-gallons of milk from giant coat pockets, no grocery bags or receipts in sight.

"It isn't fair," I agreed, crouching down. "I think—" Was I ready to put these new memories even into words? Yet it felt like the right thing to say, even though sharing it was like ripping something open and being okay with the giant hole left there.

I sat on the ground next to her as she wiped away streaks of tears with a yellow sleeve.

"I think we were poor."

Kaz lifted her eyes at me, a question on her face clearly asking how that had to do with anything.

Mrs. Trent stayed quiet, but her acerbic scent mixed into rotted waste, marking a growing fear at hearing me share these things.

I pressed my fingers against my temples, trying to access the memories. The long hours Mom was gone, working two, sometimes three shift jobs. Eating tortillas and peanut butter for three days straight.

"My Mom. She did everything she could. She didn't want to be a villain. But no one would hire her for her powers; they thought her laser vision was just destructive and couldn't help anyone. They already had strength APAs and fire APAs with better control for cutting and building and shaping. No one needed her."

Kaz had lowered her head again, hiding back inside her hood, but I heard a sniff, and I think she was listening. All smells coming from her were lightly toasted versions of the permeating odors earlier.

Mrs. Trent was standing, ever patient, keeping a steady eye on me as I spoke. Despite the fear I smelled on her, she listened intently.

"So, I guess I'm sharing this because when she first started to do what people would say is 'bad'"—I used air quotes for that word—"well, she was doing it to feed me. It hurt her to see me suffer."

A new memory developed in my mind, a birthday. Things had gotten better by then. Food was always in the house, and we even got to do fun things like those ice cream sundaes. A week before the SDF had come, Mom handed me a box covered in blue wrapping paper for my birthday. A PlayStation that came with three games. I would only ever get to play one.

"I saved for months," her face had beamed at me as I began opening the large box, too excited to register the citrusy scent filling the room was a sign of her lying.

I bent down to see if Kaz would meet my eye. "She started doing those things to help me. She loved me." I blinked as the painful memory seared my senses with that metallic scent. Being pulled away as I heard my mother scream. "They only saw a villain. They never saw a mom just trying to survive.

"This place isn't perfect, but it can help you be *you*. And when you realize you don't have to keep fighting every day to prove yourself, when you are in a place where you can be safe and your needs are met, you have the space to learn to be your best self. To choose instead of be controlled."

Kaz looked at me, waiting for me to fill in the rest, but I let the unspoken question hang as we looked at each other.

What do you choose?

Mrs. Trent finally moved, purposefully. Ignoring how uncomfortable it probably was in her skirt, she sat next to us on the blacktop.

"Miss Elloy." Her voice is melodic, transfixing even when not making demands. "Do you know my ability?"

Kaz nods. The other kids probably told her. The fact that someone as powerful as she was here and not locked up in an SDF cell gained her a lot of respect from the students. Hella respect from me.

"When I was ten, my brother destroyed my favorite book. So, I told him to take the kitchen shears from the kitchen, cut off his pinky, then eat it. So he did."

Kaz and I look at each other. I tried not to allow that mental image in my head.

"When the SDF came, they tased me and put me in a cell. I was gagged and not allowed to speak. I was angry, of course. They were taking away my control. It took another ten years of careful work in that place to realize that their fear was based on how easily I could strip them from their agency. *Their* control."

Something was lifting inside Kaz. I could smell the change as the scent around her lightened into something earthy and fresh. She understood what Mrs. Trent was saying. Choose for yourself, to stay at this school. Learn, grow, and nurture who you are. Or someone will choose for you, seeing you only for your nature and not your ability to weld it.

I stood up and held a hand out to her and Mrs. Trent.

Together, we walked into the school. The kids had been ushered back into classrooms, and I hoped my kids weren't too worried.

"I'm not sure if getting you back to class is the best thing right now—" Mrs. Trent started.

Kaz stopped, looking between us. I saw a brightness in her, and in a flash, I could imagine a future Kaz, who like Mrs. Trent, had figured out her control. She would mess up again, maybe nearly blow us all up in the process, but she'd accepted something about herself today that before she'd been rejecting. Her power. Her ability. Herself.

"Class is fine." Kaz wiped away the last of the tears she'd shed a few minutes earlier. "Danni invited me to her place after school. She said she'd memorized some weird astrology maps she thought I'd like to see."

Kaz left us, walking confidently through the cafeteria, turning down the hall back to our class.

I wiped a damp brow and assessed Mrs. Trent. She looked pleased and smelled even more relieved.

"You are so great with these kids."

I crossed my arms. "Well, you're a daily reminder of what they can be."

She nodded humbly. "I hope so." The citrusy scent hadn't left her, but it was beginning to dissipate. I waited, knowing she was about to tell me something she'd been keeping from me for some time.

"I met your mother."

She held up a finger to keep me from speaking the truckload of questions that wanted to burst from me.

"She was in the SDF cells with me, forced to wear a special eye covering."

Mrs. Trent sighed and indicated that we sit in the metal chairs I'd set out for Noah and any other kid who needed to leave the class while testing.

My mother was alive.

The volume of her scream in my memory decreased just a portion. I sat quickly but leaned forward, needing to hear more.

"They removed your memories. They do that when they remove the parents. It's supposed to keep the child from being damaged by the trauma."

An APA had taken my memories. Maybe a telepath or some other psychic ability? I was too shocked to feel angry, so I gripped the sides of the chair and listened.

"They were going to do the same to Kaz, but recently there's been an uptick in villain activity." She leaned in, and I looked into her brown eyes. "All of them were taken from homes like your own."

Kids of villains, is what she meant. Kids like me, taken from homes of known villains, then choosing villany as adults. Because their stolen memories had kept them from processing their trauma? Or because they were born to be evil? Nature or nurture, indeed.

"So," Mrs. Trent folded her hands in her lap. "Is villainy bred or learned? You know that at Autonomy High School, we teach that agency trumps both of those things, and I hold to that."

I nodded quietly. Even now, I had to believe that my future was my choice, despite my DNA, despite even my experiences, though my choices were often shaped by them. What choices would I have made differently had I kept the memory of Mom, the years of deprivation coupled with the knowledge that I had a parent who would do anything to care for me? Or maybe it didn't matter because I'd been lucky enough to be put in the home of kind, adoptive parents who had supported and cared for me.

"But—" Mrs. Trent continued, "—I believe we are doing these children a disservice by taking away their choice to remember. Even something horrible."

Mrs. Trent's voice broke as she said the last word, and I realized she must be thinking of what she did to her brother. That memory had taught her the frightening might of her ability and kept her careful every day she opened her mouth now.

We parted ways in the hall as I rejoined my class. Spencer was flying circles on the ceiling while Noah and Chet tried to throw some kind of candy into his open mouth. Chet's strength had created a few candy-shaped craters in the ceiling.

Things were back to normal, but I could feel that hard spot twisting inside.

Letting the kids entertain themselves for a minute, I stepped back out into the hallway as the emotions churning inside me expanded, tightening my throat, clenching my jaw. Down the hall was an empty counselor's office. As soon as I shut the door behind me, I crumpled in a mess of heaving breaths, every tightly wound emotion over the past hour finally releasing.

As tears streamed down my face, I let everything I'd rediscovered about Mom flood me with every feeling I'd ever categorized. Pain at how she was treated, indignance for the unfairness of her efforts to work within the system, anger that she felt forced to then work outside of it. Utter grief at how she was taken from me and the hole that was left because of it. Betrayal at a system that had both helped me and ripped any memory of my mother from me.

As my body rid itself of these thoughts, expelling them like poisoned food, I began to breathe normally again. Weariness washed over my body, but that hard pit was gone, and as I wiped my face and pulled myself off the dark, industrial carpet, I felt lighter than I had in years.

A flowery smell greeted me as I returned to class a few minutes later. Suni, more often invisible than visible, was in a happy mood. I heard her breathy laugh while watching the boys as Spencer was now collecting the candy from the ceiling, and Troy and Chet were yelling he should share it.

Danni and Kaz were sitting at the front row table, probably making plans for the evening.

I was glad to see no one was acting weird around Kaz. Everyone here had bad days, even destructive ones.

"Okay, folks," I said loud enough to get their attention. Spencer sunk into his chair, though I knew he wouldn't stay in it for long.

Noah had spent the entire time constructing something out of wires and a battery, and a red light was now flashing in his hand. He looked up. "Hey, Mr. E, I think I figured out how those SDF tasers work—"

A beam of electricity shot from Noah's contraption and created a smoking, black spot in the dead center of the smart board. The class erupted in a mix of cheers.

As the metallic, ozone smell hit me, the last piece of my mother's face became clear. Her intense eyes were focused on me, her curly hair wild and free. She'd tried so hard, and in the end, she chose to use her power to give me a better life. In the end, she actually had.

She was still alive. I was going to find her, and maybe even figure out how to make her feel safe enough to feel in control again.

MERMAID'S JUSTICE

INNA V. LYON

Science Fiction Short Story

Rooza, April of the current year

"*R*ooza, get back to your aquarium." Tina slammed her palm on the walnut desk. "You are dripping filthy water on my Persian rug."

Pffft! Rooza let out a wet exhale. Persian rug! It was a colorful carpet with big green sea cucumbers covering the tiles.

Have you forgotten, Tina, that water dries?

In Tina's defense, her office was expensive. And Tina, currently, was fuming on the throne of her palace or a museum. Or a prison.

Two thousand square feet of Italian marble and sandalwood, with a collection of furniture and decor that could adorn a palace—it was clear her business was doing well. After Tina had added trophies and showpieces to office decorations, it became the envy of any museum. What curator wouldn't love to get their hands on an exhibit of ancient wooden masks from the Congo, a collection of authentic New Guinea spears and bows, or a replica of a Moai statue from Easter Island? And then there was the aquarium, large enough for the only mermaid in captivity.

Yes, Rooza was a real mermaid. Caught in the Barents Sea near Russia, she was classified as a Russian trophy, though she didn't speak the language. Most of the words and phrases she knew were snippets of fishermen's conversations in different languages. "Fish" in English, "pesce" in Italian, "vis" in Dutch, and a handful of what she assumed were Russian swear words. First, she didn't want to speak. Second, she couldn't. She'd ruptured her vocal cord, screaming for hours while caught in plastic fishing nets polluting the ocean.

She didn't have a real name, either. Outside of captivity, mermaids didn't spend their time together too often. Her captors referred to her as "rusalka," the Russian word for mermaid. Over time, it shortened to "Rooza," and it stuck.

Here's a show for you, Tina, Rooza thought bitterly.

Rooza dove back into the water, pretending to drown, faking choking, rolling her eyes, and pressing her hands to her gills. Rooza couldn't tell if Tina's face showed more boredom or annoyance. Rooza zipped to the surface in one swift movement and leaped to the aquarium's small platform decorated with a replica of a Copenhagen gray stone. Rooza gulped for air. She could stay underwater for hours, but the temptation was too great to miss. She wanted to put on a show to irritate Tina, just what that devil of a woman deserved. As Rooza ran her tail through the water, another massive wave of water splashed on the rug, running over the tiles.

Tina pressed the com button on her desk, yelling to her assistant, "Call the cleaning crew. Now!"

Clicking high heels on tile, Tina, the Vice President of a big Investment Company, stomped on the wet rug from her desk on the opposite side of the office, her eyes throwing daggers. She crossed her arms and growled in a low tone. "Don't play dumb with me. Just remember you are my property." She paused. "For now."

Rooza froze on her perch, and Tina continued. "There are multiple offers on the market. I can sell you to a private buyer who would make your life here seem like Atlantis. Many people want to buy a live mermaid for—should I say—reasons other than decoration. DNA labs, SeaWorld, exotic pet suppliers. There is even an offer from what appears to be a perverted sex shop. Shall I continue?" She gave Rooza a crooked smile. "So, tuck your tail and clean your walls. I have a special visitor tomorrow. You'd better be on your best behavior."

Rooza reached for the squeegee on the wall hook and dove in without making a splash.

She didn't doubt her time would come sooner or later. A mermaid's novelty was sure to wear off. Tina would replace her with gardening elves, mining gnomes, or any other rare object she wanted. She had the money.

Silence didn't mean defeat—Rooza needed an escape plan.

Tina, July the previous year

THAT HOT SUMMER, the Virtual Ocean Auction was full of new trendy DNA-altered and cross-bred species. The mermaid, maybe the last of her kind, was the only creature in Tina's sights. She outbid everyone for the exotic aquarium pet. She needed a stronger statement for "environmentalist business-woman" than being vegan and making donations to the Great Plastics Garbage Patch cleaning project.

Tina was excited to have this mermaid in her office. It would be the centerpiece. Tina smirked, reading the media messages positioning her as a savior of the endangered species from the toxic ocean environment; she had plenty of skeletons in her closet, but the media didn't need to know about those. As expected, there were a few protestors yelling about the cruelty of mermaid captivity, but most didn't care what Tina did with the mermaid.

After transferring hefty payments and completing the paperwork, she was dying to see her new acquisition.

"I want the best aquarium service this city has to offer," she told her assistant.

San Bernardino Aqua Life company installed a fish tank the size of a medium vertical swimming pool in Tina's office in a week. In another week, two middle-aged men, one an Aqua Technician and the other a Certified Aquatic Veterinarian, fussed about water temperature, filtration system, leakage, and every plant. The third week, Tina fantasized violence toward the two men who announced the water needed more time to cycle through and stabilize. She gave them a piece of her mind right then.

Her precious and long-anticipated cargo would be delivered the next day, but the two shaken men in blue uniforms kept muttering about dissolved gasses, the percentage of heavy metals, and the aquarium's pH level. Tina didn't bother to remember their names, referring to them as Bill and Bob in her mind and addressing them in the plural.

"You idiots! I want this ready by tomorrow."

She shoved the investment portfolio folder to the edge of her desk, knocking the bio-grade paper cup filled with ice water flying toward the two pale men. Bob flinched, and Bill kneeled to collect the cubed ice, muttering, "We will try."

An hour later, they brought her a tablet displaying a document that declared in fine print, "The aquarium water contained here will support live species."

Tina smiled and signed.

Four weeks later, Bill and Bob were back.

Rooza, August of the previous year

ROOZA HEARD fishermen talking about their homes on the land. Her home was vast, beautiful, filled with the cry of seagulls and the indistinct smell of salt mixed with seaweed and iodine. She missed it.

The salty water of the Barents Sea turned murky and stinky on the third day in Rooza's transportation pod. She shared her container with a fresh bycatch from the same region—a few families of cod, haddock, pollock, and one king crab. Despite the others in the pod, Rooza was lonely and scared. And angry. The others didn't last long. Rooza didn't disdain seafood, even though she mostly ate seaweed and algae, so when left without a choice, she ate all her fellow prisoners by the end of the fifth day. All except the crab. He was feisty and survived Rooza's attacks. She was proud of the crab.

Her appetite grew to the point of no mercy by the voices, the darkness, and her fear of the unknown. The mechanical noises of the massive fishing vessel didn't help. The crab didn't survive after day seven.

When sailors lifted the pod's lid, the stench of ammonia and nitrite broke free, inciting gasps of disgust. Two sailors covered their noses with palms.

"Holy mackerel! What did she do?"

"She ate them all, you dummy, and then she pooped just like we do, except she didn't have a toilet."

After that incident, the sailors changed the pod's water daily and fed her one big fish a day, leaving the top covered with fish-net. Fresh cod curbed her appetite but didn't lift her spirit. The rocking of the ship and the smell of the ocean made her more restless. Freedom was so close and so far.

The ship docked in a Los Angeles port a week later.

Rooza didn't remember much about the journey and her ending in a spacious tank in Tina's office. Possibly a sedative in her food had put her into a deep sleep. She felt soft sand on her back and kelp seaweed brushing her body. She drifted into a dream of the sea—chasing fish and playing with other mermaids—but the pungent smell of chemicals hit her nostrils, and Rooza jerked up.

Where am I? Who are they?

Behind the thick glass wall, dozens of people stared at her, pointing their fingers, flashing their cameras, raising their drinks, laughing, and talking gibberish.

Scared and confused, Rooza locked eyes with the woman in the middle of the crowd. A petite blonde in high heels and a blue suit stood immovable with her arms crossed and her face unreadable. Rooza pressed her webbed hands against the tank wall. She knew this human was in charge and could change her destiny.

Help. Let me out. I don't belong here and never will, Rooza begged with desperate eyes. Her mouth kept moving, letting air bubbles out. Her pink gills flapped rapidly in unison with her palpitating heart. She would have fainted if she knew how.

The woman turned her back and walked away.

Her emotions in disarray, Rooza swam up and down, fighting for the woman's attention. She banged her fist against the wall of the tank. Once, twice, ten times. The banging elicited more laughter and picture-snapping from the crowd.

The woman never looked back. Rooza swore she would never trust a human again.

Tina, September of the previous year

TINA TYPED "MERMAID BEHAVIOR IN CAPTIVITY" into a search engine—no articles or research studies popped up, only legends and fantasy movies. What did she expect? Recipe books for a mermaid's diet?

True, she'd hoped for a well-behaved fish to put in her enormous aquarium to compliment her office, business, and public image. She even prepared a joke for her visitors. "What is the opposite of a mermaid? A landlady!"

Aside from the annoying chemical aquarium smell, her new fish had bigger problems and an even bigger personality than Tina needed. The brainless wet thing kept banging the tank glass, rushing up and down like mad, splashing water out of the tank, and making annoying gurgling noises.

"I shouldn't be a Vice President of a multimillion-dollar investment company if I can't tame a Russian mermaid," she told herself. Leaving Rooza without food for three days over Labor Day weekend would teach this fish a lesson.

Upon returning to the office, Tina found Rooza at the bottom of the tank. The mermaid acted indifferent to anything, even to fresh cod.

"Are you going to behave now? Be a good—" Tina almost said "fish" but at the last second changed it to "girl." Rooza flipped her tail and moved into a corner, turning her silver body away from Tina.

Tina cursed all sea life under her breath.

The following day, Tina entered her office and wrinkled her nose. The filet of cod was still on the platform, untouched, dried, and filling the office with the smell of rotting fish. Rooza hung near the surface, gasping for air. Her gills changed color from pink to blood-red. Veins pulsated through spots of transparent skin free of scales.

Tina knocked on the glass. "Hey, what is going on?"

Rooza's gills moved rapidly, and her limp body sank to the bottom of the aquarium. Tina had to call those two idiots to check on her specimen.

Bill and Bob arrived in record time. One of them—probably Bill—offered in an exasperated voice, "Rooza is significant organic matter, and she produces, well, organic waste.

The water has ammonia poisoning, and it offset the nitrogen cycle."

"Fix it, then. Add more chemicals. Change the water. Do what you were hired to do," Tina snapped.

Bill opened his mouth. "It is not that simple anymore. Your," he stuttered. "Your aquarium inhabitant is sick now."

"She is a fish. Just a big stupid fish." Tina didn't expect her voice to shriek. "Give her some pills and make her well."

Bob, who was probably the vet, took a determined step toward her desk—a muscle tic developing in his jawline—and proceeded in a firm voice that made Tina want to slap him.

"I've never treated a fish that size. I don't know her physiology and health history. If I treat her as I would guppies or tetras, she might die."

"What do you suggest?"

"We need a specialist. I know someone who can help."

Clenching and unclenching her fists under the table, Tina closed her eyes and counted to five. "Make the call."

A couple of hours later, a lean, gorgeous young woman stormed into the office, spent a few minutes observing listless Rooza, and marched to Tina's desk.

"Helena Mendez, Catalina Island Essential Fish Habitat marine biologist." She looked in her late twenties, dark shiny hair in a thick ponytail and sun-kissed Mexican heritage skin.

"What's wrong with my fish?"

Tina didn't like Helena—for her youth, beauty, the confidence in her voice, or her daring manners.

Helena rose her brow. "Your live specimen is very ill. Rooza suffered damage to her immune system from exposure to a high level of nitrite. Her methemoglobin level increased, and she is now prone to fin rot disease. You are fortunate I came today. Another day or two, and she would have sustained permanent damage to her liver, possibly causing death."

Tina glanced at the Forbes magazine featuring her as an

endangered species savior and shivered. If a mermaid died on her watch, her public image as a sea life preservationist would plummet to the bottom of that damn aquarium.

"What do you suggest we do?"

"We have a lot of work ahead of us. Clean the tank and refill it with Reverse Osmosis water, add some marine salt and new chemicals, and use medication and diet variation to heal Rooza. I will need space and time."

"Do whatever you need to." Tina paused. "Please, keep her alive." She should've added an emotional "Thank you" as well. Instead, she waved her hand, dismissing Helena, and turned to her computer.

Tina checked the company website and her social media page. Both already had comments about the marine biologist's visit and speculations about a sick mermaid in captivity.

Tina typed Helena's name and title in the search browser. A few dozen articles about the ocean's environmental impact on Earth popped up on the Fish Habitat website and in other scientific magazines.

Great, another day or two, and Tina would have an angry crowd in front of her building with posters like "Free Rooza," "Protect the ocean—leave it alone," or "Women's rights for mermaids." It was hard to be rich and righteous at the same time.

Rooza, December of the last year

FOR ROOZA, days meshed into weeks of secluded life in a metal container and Helena's company. The memories of painful needles poking her body and a forced transfer into a smaller tank didn't build Rooza's trust in Helena.

The slender, tanned woman was there every day for hours on end, boring Rooza with stats and numbers. Helena concealed the aquarium surroundings with plastic curtains—making Rooza claustrophobic—and populated the area with pumps, filters, and rows of containers with chemicals.

Rooza watched Helena checking water parameters or typing on her laptop. It was all she could do—observe the marine biologist at work.

Rooza's diet consisted of small portions of raw fish to aid recovery, but one day, Helena brought her something green, placing it on the edge of the container.

Was it Green Algae? She missed the ocean and fresh food so much.

Rooza touched the leaves with her webbed hand. The two leaves were not algae. Yes, they were green, but they had wrinkled veins and smelled funny.

"It's cabbage," Helena said.

She moved her chair closer to the tank and turned her laptop to show Rooza the screen. Image after image revealed the story of cabbage—how it grew, was harvested, and used as food. Helena talked in a soft tone, explaining some of the pictures and pointing out details that sea inhabitants wouldn't know. Rooza listened with intent but distrust, expecting Helena to lure a poor mermaid into more pain.

Instead, Helena took one cabbage leaf, shrugged her shoulders, and ate it. Rooza snatched the second leaf, content with the display, and dove to the bottom of the tank, where she took her first bite. The texture was fibery and the taste was bittersweet but crunchy and fresh. She finished it all and returned to the surface.

"Did you like it? Want more?" Helena took the whole head of cabbage out of her gray canvas bag. "Vegetables are good for you. I'm a vegetarian and eat plant-based food, but don't worry, I won't keep you from your fish."

Helena smiled and tore a couple more cabbage leaves to

share. She had no idea how much Rooza missed the greens in her diet.

Their food adventure continued every day. Helena would bring carrots, apples, celery sticks, and Brussel sprouts, share them, and show a presentation on her laptop. Hesitant at first, Rooza soon bounced on her tail in anticipation of Helena's visit, the new foods, and lessons. She learned about the human world and its customs. Money ruled most of that weird world, and people like Tina were on the top of the food chain. Not all of it was bad. Some things fascinated Rooza—children, kittens, the variety of food, and entertainment.

Rooza wished she could satisfy Helena's curiosity about her own home. She would tell her of the multifaceted life of the incredible ocean, its inhabitants, freedom, the beauty of colors, danger, and fishery predators roaming the sea in their death machine vessels.

One afternoon, she found a way to communicate with her new friend.

Helena left her laptop on the chair near the metal tank while checking the aquarium's chemicals. Rooza reached the keyboard and typed a word with clumsy fingers, leaving wet prints on the black surface.

Rooza watched the marine biologist's forehead wrinkle when she found what Rooza had typed.

FISHEGGS.

Helena raised her eyebrows and dropped her chin. "Fish eggs? Do you want some caviar? Can you read and type? That's really amazing."

Helena rubbed her temples, took a few deep breaths, and turned the machine to Rooza with a blank document on the screen and a hopeful expression on her face.

"How old are you?" Helena asked.

"MANY WINTERS." Rooza typed.

"Do you have a family?"

"DIDN'T SEE THEM LONG TIME."
Rooza's world didn't seem so lonely anymore.

Tina, April of the current year

TINA HATED pretending to be a vegan and sustainable-living enthusiast. She grimaced at her spinach smoothie in a biodegradable cup and pressed the twelfth floor on the elevator dash. Her stomach twisted every time she had to order from a vegan menu at dinner parties. All she wanted was a veal saltimbocca and yellowfin tuna sushi.

Her public eco-image asked for too many sacrifices. She could pull it off if she kept her secrets. Who was here to reveal them to the world?

A vegan lifestyle of the caliber that she was 'living' required avoiding clothing derived from animals. Besides craving meat and fish, Tina had another passion that would've destroyed her eco-friendly image in a blink. She loved everything from leather to fur and couldn't stop buying top brands of apparel and accessories—she enjoyed possessing what others couldn't have. It made her feel powerful.

Unfortunately, that power was locked behind a password-protected metal door in her office, leading to a spacious walk-in closet. There she kept her priceless, damning possessions. Her security system was very reliable, even better than at her house. She had only five fur coats—no one needs more than that, especially if you live in California. The genuine leather handbag obsession she harbored was a different story. Five massive display cabinets lined the perimeter of the closet, hiding Tina's high-brand handbag and clothing collections.

Custom-made Louis Vuitton purses with matching luggage, artisan saddle-stitched Hermeses, calf BVLGARI totes of various colors, Wilson's leather jacket and purse sets, lambskin vintage Channel, Salvatore Ferragamo patent clutches, and countless other bags filled the space behind the tempered-glass door displays.

The jewel of her collection was the Black Diamond handbag by Birkin.

The waiting list for Birkin's products was larger than myth, and Tina had to jump through a few hoops to collect it. She secretly flew to Paris just to buy the 35-inch alligator black skin handbag with diamond closure for 250,000 Euros.

Why she had to have so many handbags, she wouldn't be able to explain even to her therapist. Animal Rights Movements decried animal cruelty, carnivorous diets, and animal materials in clothing for decades now. She couldn't wear her incriminating fur coats or travel with her luxurious $60K luggage in public, but possessing them was enough.

One April Sunday morning, Tina drove to the office to expose her handbag to the sun for a quarter-hour to keep it safe from mold and fungus.

Her private elevator delivered her to her office, where she found Helena Mendez with bottles of chemicals and filters spread all over the floor. Tina forgot she'd allowed Helena to research Rooza for her dissertation on the third Sunday of the month.

Tina's mouth fell open when she saw Rooza sitting on the platform and holding Helena's laptop.

"Am I the only one who is seeing the mermaid in the room typing on the computer?"

Helena stood up, her eyes wide and worried. "Rooza doesn't talk. But she can read. She asked for food by typing caviar on my laptop."

"Is she ordering food now? Is that why my monthly bills doubled? My fish is eating caviar?"

Helena replied in a calm demeanor. "Yes, caviar is an excellent source of protein, calcium, and phosphorus. You asked me to save her life, and that's what I'm doing—feeding her a high-protein diet. The laptop is our way to communicate."

Tina narrowed her eyes and pursed her lips. "I allowed you to come here for your research. I agreed to the middle-school students' field trips as part of an educational program. I spend thousands of dollars maintaining this stinky aquarium in my office, and now you are teaching my fish to ask for caviar on a laptop?"

Helena's face turned red. "She is not a fish. She is a smart and brave person who had life and family in the ocean before you made her another exhibit for your museum display."

"She is my commodity, and a very expensive one. Your research is over." Tina made a sweeping gesture. "Collect your belongings and get out of here." She marched toward the walk-in closet. "Don't forget to turn your badge in."

Tina punched in the code and slammed the door before drawing in a slow, steady breath. A burst of nervous laughter escaped her chest. There were a few empty spaces on one of the cabinet shelves. A silvery mermaid-skin handbag would make a unique addition to her collection. Too bad no one would ever see it.

Rooza, current year, the first week of May

THE OBLONG-SHAPED white pill rolled on Rooza's palm. She closed her fist and eyes.

Three days ago, when Tina fired the marine biologist, Helena gave Rooza her security badge and a tiny jar with a single pill inside.

"I wish I could do more for you, Rooza. But my time here is over. Now your destiny will be up to you. This is an experimental pill I got from the black market. It contains calcium and engineered elements capable of changing DNA. It would be dangerous to take it without my supervision, but you might have to take that risk if you want to get out of here."

Rooza's tears fell into the aquarium's salty water. She'd lost her only friend.

Rooza had hidden the glass jar and plastic badge on top of the aquarium filter but hesitated to take the pill. Without Helena, Rooza's world shrank back to four walls with the side-view of Tina's closet and the future with a sense of impending doom. Was the DNA pill her only solution? What would happen to her?

She made her decision after Tina's special visitor arrived. A talkative young man almost danced when he saw Rooza and kept saying, "Ariel, dye her hair red, sea-shell bra," and other nonsense.

Their parting conversation tipped the scale for Rooza.

"And how are you going to present the news to the world?" asked the young man.

"Don't worry about that. I already prepared a fake press release, including pictures of her released into the sea. In a couple of days, I have an exclusive broadcast with a popular morning channel. No one will question her absence. Make sure you modify her appearance and tell the media it is a DNA-altered version and not a real specimen."

Rooza pushed away all her doubts and fears, unclenched her fist, and swallowed the pill.

The next day, her fins itched. She rubbed her hands over the itchy spot and came across a poorly attached flap of discolored flakes.

Was she sick again? Her skin itched, and her tail hurt.

She brushed her body again. To her horror, the large patch of lighter skin below her knees peeled off like a filet. Underneath it, in oozing liquid, she saw two skinny legs with veins pulsating in unison with her fast-beating heart.

Was that what DNA means? Turning into a human? Growing legs?

She wished Helena were there to answer her questions and tell her if the leg effect was permanent. But she was alone, facing uncertain times and changes in her body.

With trepidation, she covered her legs again, and silvery skin stuck back to her body with a wet slap. Flakes produced a slimy substance and sealed the seam, oozing some blood. At least it healed fast.

Rooza braced herself and didn't touch her body for the rest of the day despite her itchy skin and the heavy weight of her tail.

Curiosity took over in the evening after Tina left the office.

Rooza climbed onto the platform and peeled the skin off from hip to tail. The chunk of fins and tails slid off into the aquarium like a pair of silky pants—two perfect human legs dangled from the platform. She admired them and touched her little pink toes.

She had legs, so she could walk, and she could leave that place. She only needed clothes and a security pass. Thank you, Helena.

She jumped from the platform and landed in a heap on the Persian rug with sea cucumbers. The first few steps were painful and unstable, but after an hour of practice and steadying herself with the furniture, Rooza mastered shaky walking skills. She approached the walk-in closet and typed the password she saw Tina typing many times: landlady25. The metal door opened with a soft click. The rows of cabinets with clothes and handbags glistened in the dark.

Tina, current year, the first week of May

THE *GOOD MORNING, California* filming crew arrived early, waiting on the first floor with their cameras and anchorman.

Traffic made Tina five minutes late. She hated being late. She waved to the crew with a free hand, then clutched her new Mark Cross eco-tote made of recycled materials on her shoulder. The other hand held a disgusting green smoothie. The producer and anchorman greeted her and piled into her private elevator. Tina pressed the twelfth-floor button. The crew was already filming the busy morning of the Vice President, legend of the investment market, eco-altruist of sustainable living.

"I did my restorative yoga this morning and confirmed a couple of charitable events with my assistant," chirped Tina. "Scheduled my lunch at the new plant-based restaurant and—"

The elevator door pinged, and the crowd stepped into Tina's office. Silence echoed off the walls. Bright-colored handbags, totes, and purses of all imaginable colors and brands populated the floor, couches, and Tina's desk. The famous black gator purse, diamonds sparkling, was sprawled on the bottom of the aquarium, ruined forever.

Her mink coat enveloped the Moai Easter Island statue, and a sable hat with two bushy tails crowned the top. The four other fur coats curled on the floor like sleeping kittens.

All Tina could utter was, "It's not mine."

The cameras kept rolling.

The anchorman's voice didn't sound convincing. "Your company website released the news about freeing Rooza last night? Is it true?"

Rooza, current year, the first week of May

A SELF-DRIVING taxi pulled into the empty parking lot of the Parker's Lighthouse restaurant in Long Beach. Five o'clock in the morning was too early for guests. Rows of private boats glistened in the distance. As Rooza turned to face the ocean, the smell of home welcomed and overwhelmed her.

Rooza took a short walk to the end of the public pier, rolling a suitcase behind her. The LV leather luggage did an excellent job of keeping her tail moist and preserved.

At the end of the pier, she spread the tailed skin on the hard concrete. Then, she shed her human clothes, sat down, placed her delicate legs inside the skin, and flipped the edges. As soon as silvery flakes touched her body, the sealing effect took over and enclosed her legs in a tight cocoon with fins and tail. A few dried scales stuck to the interior of the abundant luggage.

Rooza didn't know if she was destined to stay human or mermaid. Obviously, the reversal effect of the DNA pill from human to mermaid and back won't last forever, but until it did, Rooza had a plan to put its magic to work.

Before jumping from the pier, she looked back at the city where the human world was waking up.

Helena had explained to Rooza about the damaged ocean's ecosystems, sea piracy, illegal fishing, whales and dolphins slaughter, bycatch statistics, and government subsidiaries. But she also told Rooza about ocean activists' movements, beach cleaning volunteers, Sea Shepherd's forces, proactive companies, and people who cared about the future of the ocean and the planet.

Now all she needed to do was to find other mermaids and band together to fight for a clean home. Helena said, "Good deeds start with someone. Just one. Look in the mirror."

Rooza inhaled the ocean. The smell of salt, iodine, and freedom filled her nostrils and chest. She looked at her reflection in the seawater and took a long-anticipated dive.

PLUMS AND CHERRIES

K. HERRING

Poem

Two blossoms came to greet me; they came in different
  time
Most wouldn't see the difference
If I held them side by side

When in times of sorrow, one would near abide
Although he had to leave me
He was there when I had cried

Another came in gladness, its leaves were evergreen
I sat with him in sunshine
And told him where I'd been

Seasons come and seasons go
But can we stay the same?

Will weathered roots breed sturdy trees
And will sturdy trees remain?

Two blossoms came to greet me, in Winter and in
   Spring
I walked beneath their arbors
And listened to them sing.

Will you come back to see me? I asked within my heart
A lonely child worried
About being far apart.

Remember not with sadness, or think you can't be found
A fruit cannot be seeded
Until its fallen to the ground

Though memories fade and pass away
In darkness they retreat

The scent of flowers lingers on
And always smells as sweet

THE HUMBLE EARTHWORM

VALARIE SCHENK

Personal Memoir

I walked out the front door on a drizzly afternoon with the intention to fetch the mail but, instead, stood still—my hand holding the door wide open—while my mind flooded with memories. So powerful were the images; it was like stepping into a time machine. Smell does that—draws us back in time—to days long forgotten. And so it was on this day. There, on the porch, my forty-seven-year-old self inhaled crisp air—ripe with moist petrichor as the clouds broke and rain subsided. The once dry yard was now dotted with damp pockets of deeply nourished and pleasantly fragrant soil. I lingered there for a moment, lungs full, mind wandering to the past. Then let it all go. On my exhale, I was young again, stooping low to the ground in my favorite childhood play space.

I was ten years old or so, inquisitive, experimental, shy, but fearless in my natural settings. I spent hours outside my child-hood home digging deep into sod-bare soil. I was long past serving up decadent mud pies and decorative fairy cakes heaped with sun-faced dandelions. Gone, too, were the intricate earthen carvings of roadways, canals, rivers, vast lakes, and mountain vistas. Yet I kept digging and certainly not just for the sake of habit. No. I prided myself as a scientist. Equipped with a blade-like shovel, I sunk tool after tool into rich earth in order to uncover mysteries buried deep. With wide eyes and swollen ego, I exhumed bottle caps, glass shards, and the occasional orbed marble, undoubtedly owned by mystical wizards of long ago. Additionally, I encountered serpentine abodes of hard-working ants and healthy caches of infamously gentle roly-polies. I continued my labors, hoping to cross paths with the prized being, Charles Darwin himself, who so admired the worm. Said he, "Without the work of this humble creature, who knows nothing of the benefits he confers upon mankind, agriculture, as we know it, would be very difficult if not wholly impossible." Despite its small stature and perceived lowly station in life, I knew I was to approach this organism with reverence. Starstruck, I carried on my search. It was during one such endeavor that tragedy arose. Yes. My garden spade hit an earthworm.

Mortified, I knelt, frozen, before the halved creature. I let tears wash the soil from its body as I tenderly lifted each piece. With love, I caressed its grooved skin, then transferred one half to my left hand, the other half to my right. Glancing from one hand to the next, I sobbed.

Shame-faced and head-dropped, I dragged my feet into my bedroom. Click. With the door now securely latched behind me, I mournfully confined myself to bed, where I interned the lifeless worm safely, but temporarily, under my pillow. Hands clenched around thick headboard slats, I peered longingly through imagined prison bars. Guilt had left me paralyzed. I didn't know what to do.

Hours passed, or so it seemed. The tears had long stopped.

Sorrow eased. Resolute, I promised I would never again commit such a heinous crime. Furthermore, I had an idea. I knew just how to help out my wounded friend. The studying began. Construction supplies emerged. My room was transformed, and the worm hospital was born.

I became obsessed, as it were, with injured earthworms. I scooped them up from garden soil, rescued them from parched concrete, and dredged them out of pristine rain puddles. Out of pure, childlike love, I gingerly transported them to my hospital for recovery. I fastidiously applied my medical expertise, trying all the remedies the ten-year-old me knew—a quick wash, a Band-Aid, and a kiss. I was on cloud nine. It felt wonderful to be of service to the honorable earthworm. And so, the work went on in the shallow cardboard box heaped high with moist soil tucked proudly in a warm, dank corner of my bedroom. Only something was wrong. My plan was not working. Adjacent to my prized worm hospital, I created, out of necessity, the dreaded worm cemetery.

Day in and day out, I became sullen, morose really, as more and more patients died. Band-Aids were useless. I imagine the kisses were, too. And most frustrating were the patients that escaped, unappreciative of my services. They, as it turned out, would be found later, flattened, dry, clinging lifeless to tubular carpet fibers. Mom was ecstatic, I'm sure.

I felt hopeless. Yet I buried myself deeper into my earthworm studies. And then one day, I caught word on the playground that a worm cut in half could grow into two separate worms—alive and healthy! How was it that this information had previously eluded my attention? These words held promise. These words held hope. These words held redemption.

No longer weighed down by remorse, I returned, shovel in hand, to my backyard oasis. I plunged a sharp tip into rich loam, digging deeper, so to speak, into this new idea. Inevitably metal met an unsuspecting worm—one, and another, and yet another, repeatedly, until I finally had substantial evidence that those playground angels of mine were wrong! When digging abounds, earthworms decidedly get hurt. In fact, many die. I observed that when mercilessly chopped in half, they do not fantastically become two separate beings but rather two limp parts. No. There was no miracle that occurred before my eyes. I did learn, though, that when cut at just the right point, the "head" portion of the earthworm regenerates. Life is saved. It is these lucky and industrious earthworms that are allowed to continue with their underground careers, unseen, without accolades. Undaunted, they manage to perform their commonplace duty. And so it is that, in admiration, I ceremoniously released my noble patients to their long-awaited sanctuary. Gone was my medical career; it's true. But I didn't walk away unchanged.

As my study of the earthworm evolved, so did my knowledge of greater things. The worm's smallness taught me about the profound intricacies inherent in this world. Every creature is significant. Each organism is placed on this earth with a defined purpose. No one is a mere afterthought, not the worm and not me. To a shy young girl who often questioned her own station in life, that understanding meant everything. I think back on Darwin's words, long after the dissolution of my worm hospital and the dissipation of its organic smell, and know that he was right. Life on this planet would be very different, even difficult, without the aid of the humble earthworm, working tirelessly and hidden amid his fragrant earthy home.

THE SMELL OF BOOKS

MEGAN CONDIE

Adult Fiction

*Y*ou haven't bought a new book since before your last semester of college up until the week after your husband leaves you. Leaves you, you notice, for a woman who looks exactly like what you've always, desperately, wanted to be and now, suddenly, *aren't*.

Back then, you liked new books. You still thought you could grow up to be the heroine of a good story—blissfully ignorant of how life can seize control and bully you down paths you weren't planning on.

Embarrassed about the Young Adult dystopian novel you grab from the central display just inside the door, you murmur a word of gratitude to the literary muses that your Victorian Literature professor can't see you now.

Part of you is thinking you're not really ashamed of the book; you're ashamed of what you've done with your life. If you go any further into the store, you'll only be more intimidated by all the things you should have read in the last decade. All the places you could have gone. The things you could have done. The thinks you could have thought ...

And since you've just crossed the line into Seuss-ian ridiculousness, you go ahead and lift the intensely designed book. Parting the spine, you inhale deeply that fresh starchy scent of a new book.

The kind of scent that draws you away from the murmured voices of the store around you and into memories of yourself before you got lost in marriage and the realities of life.

The boy behind the check-out is looking at you. You put the book down. Pick it up. Give him a smile that says you're not crazy; he'll understand when he's older.

He points to the display and tells you the sequel came out just last week.

Great. Not only did you pick up popular fiction, you picked up the same popular fiction that the boy with a rock band T-shirt is reading.

You dig in your bag for your wallet before walking up to the check stand, so you won't have to stand there with your juvenile fiction on the counter while someone smart stands behind you, judging you for it.

Along the aisle for a check-out line, you see a book signing. You don't have a clue who the guy is or what he's written. In memory of the part of you who used to be informed about these things, you step over to it. First, though, you turn the book in your hand around, so the cover is facing you, not him. Hiding it from the judgment of someone who might recognize you for the fraud you are.

He grunts when you say hello.

You grunt right back. Your mother would slap you for it, but life, as you're living it today, is absurd enough to warrant it.

Some days are like that—like having your husband and his girlfriend drop in on you at work to say they're headed to

Cancun, and you'll hear from his attorney about the house. Speeding home to find he's packed his suits and favorite T-shirts but left his socks and underwear. He took the signed NFL football but left the watch you gave him for your tenth anniversary.

Car gone, phone and charger gone, engagement pictures ... *not* gone.

So, you headed out.

You put your shoes on and left. If only to prove to the spouse who was no longer there that you cared so little about his leaving that you went for a walk.

In town, you passed the hole-in-the-wall bookstore and hesitated. Confronted with a feeling that this was a sacred space you've offended every day of your life since college. You were so busy paying a mortgage and starving yourself into lingerie and making sure his home was his castle that you forgot to pay homage to the intellectualism and creativity that excited you in your youth.

Perhaps this author has written a book about a woman avenging herself on her husband.

The author lifts heavy brows—he should trim those—and heaves an exhausted sigh without even looking up at you.

Did you just grunt at him? You can't remember.

Oh, well. If Eyebrow Author gets to grunt at people, then you do, too. Just because he's got his name on the cover of a book doesn't mean he's above social etiquette. If anyone should be grunting today, it's you. This man—who's obviously living his dreams since he thinks people want his ink stain on their book—should go home and find everything he's been building for more than a decade has left him with nothing but old socks and underwear.

Perhaps ripping the pages out of the book and stomping on them while he watches would convey that feeling to him.

He says, "Where do you want it signed?"

You peek at the poster display as he's signing, and you see it's a book of his poetry.

You say, "I'm sorry I haven't heard of your work. My heart was stolen by the Gothic Victorian poets."

It's the only smart-sounding words you can string together today, and if you had to name a Gothic Victorian poet, you couldn't.

To distract from that, you add, "I don't spend much time on contemporary artists."

You tighten your fingers around the popular and mindless fiction novel in your hand, assuring yourself that no one could possibly see the cover right now and unmask your hypocrisy.

He'll like that word, *artist*. And you hope that by regurgitating terms your lit professors used, you'll sound sophisticated.

He puts the pen down and pushes the poetry book towards you on the table.

"Love is a pretty universal theme," he says. "Hopefully a little modern love poetry won't bore in comparison with those, uh, masters you read."

"Today isn't a good day for 'love.'"

You remember the Jane Austen story in which a secondary character is pining for love, and Austen's heroine tells him to read more prose because so much poetry may not be healthy.

You go ahead and retell that wise little anecdote to Eyebrow Author.

He looks up for the first time. "A cynic," he says.

"A realist," you say.

You wouldn't have said it two weeks ago, but now you have an adventure hidden in your hand and a risky sort of spite fizzling inside of you. And that starchy scent of unread books all around.

The smell of untouched pages that has been reminding you of a younger version of you since you walked in.

It might be just a little intoxicating, actually.

You had plans, then, when you were young enough to have been the hero of the adventure you clutch in your hand. You were bolder then. Confident. Life was an adventure waiting for you to conquer.

He's looking at you.

You notice the deep chocolate of his eyes. The exotic rise of cheekbones. The hint of a mystery on those full lips.

Rolling your shoulders back, you lift your chin—imitate the bold hero on the cover of the novel. If you were destined to save the world, you'd have that level of confidence, too.

A long-lost courage blossoms in your middle, taking strength with each emboldening breath you take.

You should save this man from the mediocre life he lives. You must, actually, because anyone who's going to be the hero of their own story has to seize these decisive moments if an adventure is going to be had.

You're single now, after all. The house is practically vacant. There's nothing tying you down. And here, dear hero, is the opportunity for you to choose a life-altering journey.

You'll take the poet, of course. If he is to achieve his potential, he must experience the world in a way only you can provide.

To liberate him from this small-town store, you'll first run for your car. Drive through the night to a city neither of you has ever been to. Take the first flight to a country with jungles and beaches, where you'll feed each other exotic fruits. You'll drag him out to dance in the tropical rains when he wants to take an afternoon siesta. You'll do it again in the middle of the night to gaze up at the stars and talk deeply about the meaning of life.

He'll be changed—his destiny forever altered by the soul-shattering experience you give him.

When, inevitably, you must let him return to reality and sing your siren song to someone else, he will return to the literary world with poetry that will touch the hearts and minds of any soul blessed to hear his words. The art he goes on to create will inspire, dazzle, and move people to cast aside constraints of societal expectations and the burden of misplaced responsibility and live—really *live* to such an extent that the populace of the world experiences love differently than it has in the history of the modern world.

All because you—*you*, dear hero—are brave enough to take that first step and call him away to his hero's journey.

You hold out your hand. You feel it. This moment. The portent of change. The call of destiny. The way the world is silent and waiting, unmoving as the universe around you hangs on the outcome of this moment.

Heavy from the weight of the moment, your chest tightens. You wait. Feel as if not only the masses of the earth but also the heavens hang in the balance as he decides if he will join you.

The hero meets your gaze.

Level.

Then blinks.

"You want me to sign that one too?"

The young adult novel drops from your fingers as the moment shatters around you.

He frowns as he picks up the novel from the table. You don't know if it's judgment for the young adult fantasy or the inconvenience of you dropping it.

Not that it matters. There are no heroes here. You have a mortgage to pay. Eyebrow Author has his mediocre poetry to sell.

And, let's face it, even if you were going to run off to the tropics and have a torrid affair, it wouldn't be with an author who is now—oh yes, he is indeed—signing the cover of a book he did not write.

You almost walk away, repulsed by the audacity of him signing the book you dropped. But you don't, because a moment ago, you were a different version of yourself, and you sort of—just a little bit—liked it.

Accepting the novel back from him, you don't bother thanking him.

On the way to the check out, you pick up one of everything on the end stacks that has an adventurous-looking cover.

The clerk asks if you found what you were looking for.

"Books are dangerous," you say. And you add a dozen granola bars from the impulse buy rack because you know that when you get home, you're not going to do anything except lay on the couch and read.

Made in the USA
Las Vegas, NV
10 March 2023

68840588R00118